WE'LL ALWAYS HAVE
ALCHEMY

BENEATH THE GROUND

EDITED BY JOEL LANE

A MISCELLANY OF MONSTERS

THE ALCHEMY PRESS BOOK OF HORRORS 3

Edited by PETER COLEBORN & JAN EDWARDS

THE ALCHEMY PRESS BOOK OF PULP HEROES 2

EDITED BY MIKE CHINN

The Alchemy Press Book Of Ancient Wonders

Edited by Jan Edwards & Jenny Barber

Cover art by (clockwise from top left): Jim Pitts, Danielle Serra, Dominic Harman and Les Edwards.:

WE'LL ALWAYS HAVE
ALCHEMY

Edited by

Peter Coleborn

We'll Always Have Alchemy © Peter Coleborn 2024

Cover art © Steve Upham

This publication © Alchemy Press 2024

First Edition
ISBN 978-1-911034-22-3

Published by The Alchemy Press

www.alchemypress.co.uk

CONTENTS

ACKNOWLEDGEMENTS

"Ace in the Hole" © Mike Chinn. Originally appeared in *The Paladin Mandates* (1998)

"Bones" © Adrian Tchaikovsky. Originally appeared in *The Alchemy Press Book of Ancient Wonders* (2012)

"Death and the Weaver" © Lou Morgan. Originally appeared in *The Alchemy Press Book of Urban Mythic 2* (2014)

"Dragon-Form Witch" © Joyce Chng. Originally appeared in *The Alchemy Press Book of Urban Mythic* (2013)

"Inappetence" © Steve Rasnic Tem. Originally appeared in *The Alchemy Press Book of Horrors 3* (2021)

"Lirpaloof Island" © Garry Kilworth. Originally appeared in *The Alchemy Press Book of Horrors 2* (2020)

"Meeting at the Silver Dollar" © Marion Pitman. Originally appeared in *The Alchemy Press Book of Pulp Heroes 2* (2013)

"No One Stays Dead © Bracken Macleod. Originally appeared in *The Alchemy Press Book of Pulp Heroes 3* (2014)

"Of Shadows, of Light and Dark © Jo Fletcher. Originally appeared in *Shadows of Light and Dark* (1998)

"Teufelsberg" © Madhvi Ramani. Originally appeared in *The Alchemy Press Book of Horrors* (2018)

"The Return of Boy Justice" © Peter Atkins. Originally appeared in *The Alchemy Press Book of Pulp Heroes* (2012)

"Threadbare" © Jan Edwards. Originally appeared in *Something Remains* (2016)

WE'LL ALWAYS HAVE ALCHEMY

An Introduction

I had intended this 25th anniversary anthology to appear late last year (2023). But events (dear boy) intervened (to misquote a long-gone British prime minister). And thus I am almost a year late. But better late than not at all (to misquote Geoffrey Chaucer), and so: welcome to this, our latest publication.

And while on the subject of misquotations, I must acknowledge this book's title, a nod to one of SFFH's greatest short story writers: Ray Bradbury. In case you are not sure, the title is a nod to Bradbury's story "We'll Always Have Paris", although of course this phrase can be found elsewhere, including in one of my all-time favourite movies, *Casablanca*.

Anyway, welcome to this book. *We'll Always Have Alchemy* is not intended as a "best of". That would be grossly unfair to all the fine and wonderful writers who are not included herein. Consider this volume as a "sampler". Those of a certain age may remember LPs (that's long-playing vinyl records), offering samples from the record label's oeuvre. I am reminded of albums such as *Gutbucket, You Can All Join In, Picnic, Bumpers...* (For the record [pun intended], those compilations of Top 20 hits: I don't count them.)

Therefore, in this book, in this sampler, I have selected stories from our seminal anthology titles, the various *The Alchemy Press Books Of...* series, plus one from *Something Remains* (an anthology dedicated to the memory of our late friend and supporter Joel Lane), a tale from our very first publication, the chapbook of Damian Paladin stories by Mike Chinn, and finally a poem from our first hardcover *Shadows of Light and Dark*.

Mike's collection, *The Paladin Mandates*, sporting a Bob Covington cover, was followed some months later by Jo Fletcher's poetry collection, *Shadows of Light and Dark* – both in 1998. This was all before POD made self and small-scale publishing so much easier.

Mike has been a great friend and supporter of the Press over the years, and of me too. He has edited several of our anthologies and we've published a further fine collection of his tales under our imprint. You could say that Mike is partly responsible for the past 25-plus years of publishing.

Jenny Barber and Jan Edwards have also been important editors for the Press. Especially Jan. As I type these words, she is ploughing through all our publications ensuring that the appendices are not lacking names (any omissions, though, are of course my responsibility). Pop along to these pages now for a complete list of our titles and contributors.

The Alchemy Press is basically a one-man show, although others (again I'm mostly thinking Jan here) have provided invaluable assistance in editing in all senses of the word. That's why we have a limited repertoire; and as age continues to creep up, we'll publish fewer titles still. But look at the quality, the variety. The name "Alchemy" was deliberately chosen to highlight the range of science fiction, fantasy and horror, and non-fiction that we publish.

Why the Alchemy Press? In the 1980s and 1990s my "fan" activity was centred on the British Fantasy Society and its annual convention Fantasycon. I spent my time on the society's committees, in various roles, helping to organise the convention, and editing a number of BFS publications including *Dark Horizons* and *Chills*. In the late 1990s, with projects in mind that I knew the BFS schedule wasn't geared up for, I took advantage of lottery funding available at the time and struck out on my own as a small press publisher.

Also, there were relatively few UK publications accepting short stories, especially horror and dark fantasy, from fledgling British writers. Since I much prefer shorter fiction over novels, I wanted to provide a small home where such stories could see print. Back then, writers had to send printed copies of their manuscripts to editors (along with an ssae) which made it more burdensome for Brits to get published in the USA.

Nowadays, instant communications and electronic submissions have drastically altered the life of the writer and editor. Instant communications does have an unintended consequence: during the submission windows hundreds of stories flood in ... but that's another story.

Before I end this Introduction, I must also add the

names of a few who have provided on-going support in these endeavours over the past quarter of a century: Stephen Jones, David Sutton, Jo Fletcher, Trevor Kennedy; as well as Alchemy's editors Jan Edwards, Jenny Barber, Mike Chinn, Allen Ashley, Dean Drinkel, Pauline Dungate, and of course the much-missed Joel Lane.

In fact, to all the writers and artists listed in the appendices: this book is a thank you to you all.

Peter Coleborn
Publisher The Alchemy Press
July 2024

DEDICATION

For Jan, without whom none of this would have happened.

TEUFELSBERG

Madhvi Ramani

As soon as I got off the train, I knew I was right about the story. The station was small. One platform. One waiting room. One sign held up by two twisted iron posts: Teufelsberg.

Herr Koch climbed off after me with his bags of knives. He was long and thin, all angular features and crisp shirt lapels. I had heard of people resembling their pets, but their jobs? Then again, here I was in a frayed trench coat looking as shabby as a thumbed tabloid. Your typical disgraced hack. We wished each other *Aufwiedersehen* and agreed to have a beer together if our paths crossed again.

"You always meet a person two times in life," he said in accented English and I vaguely recalled my German grandmother saying something similar.

He wasn't the type I normally drank with. There was something old-fashioned about him even though he couldn't have been more than forty. Still, we had made small talk upon boarding the train together in Berlin.

"Then to Nurnberg, down to Munich and into Austria..." he had said outlining his schedule.

"Must be difficult being away from home so much,"

I replied.

"Yes, it is. Although sometimes I think it is better being on the road where I have the comfort of warm thoughts of home. It is never so satisfying when I get there. Sebastian locks himself away with his computer. Anna is so bossy even though she is only seven and my wife does not even…"

He chuckled realising he had overstepped the boundaries of polite train conversation. I smiled and nodded to help him out, then he looked out of the window while I browsed the day's stories on my laptop. He had proven the perfect travelling companion. My old journalism professor's words echoed in my head: *Don't burn your bridges; you never know when you might need a contact.* It was unlikely I'd ever need a quote from a German knives salesman but I took his card anyway.

"Be sure to catch your train," I said.

His grey eyes flashed with amusement. *Facetious American.* He had almost an hour before his connecting train to Erfurt but I knew something he didn't: an uncanny number of people had gone missing from this station. People just passing through or waiting for their connecting trains, like Herr Koch.

A couple of cast iron cauldrons overflowing with marigolds stood at either side of the entrance to the station. Bright red. Flourishing oddly out of season. They glowed as if pulsing with heat, like a wound against the bleak sky.

A cello's mournful melody drifted out of a window and accompanied me down the main road. I stopped at the first *Pension* I saw, lingering at the door to hear the rest of the tune but it abruptly stopped. I sighed and entered a dark lobby making a bell tinkle. The room smelt of warm wood. A goth with black hair and dark eyes, wearing clinking silver bracelets, appeared. She didn't exactly fit in with her quaint German surroundings.

I deposited my bag in the single room – it was standard fare, flowery bed sheets, dinky bathroom – and went down for an early dinner of goulash and *semmel knoedel*. I sat at the table and opened my folder of notes. A newspaper clipping fluttered out. I picked it up.

It was the short article that had started this whole escapade. A fluff piece by Maria Weimann about a man who had gone missing, last seen getting off at Teufelsberg even though it wasn't his stop. His wife had followed in an attempt to find him but she too had disappeared. I didn't think of it again until a few weeks later; the same paper noted the death of the journalist who had written the story – Maria Weimann. That's when I got that feeling, that tingling at the back of my neck, that alerts me to a story.

I looked into it. You can't trust everything you read. I knew better than most. I got in touch with an old Berlin correspondent under the pretence of looking to get back into the game and he grudgingly put me in touch with someone at the same newspaper group. When I called her, she told me there were no jobs and she couldn't help me, but you don't spend over ten years being a journalist without learning how to push.

We met for a coffee. Her lips were so pursed her face creased. My reputation had preceded me.

I asked her banal questions about company structures, editors and freelancers until about thirty-five minutes in when we were almost done – because that's when you hit them with the real question – I said I was sorry to hear about the recent death of her colleague. Her lips loosened at that. She revealed that Weimann had collapsed in a bar in Teufelsberg from alcohol poisoning. That tingle again. How many deaths were caused by alcohol poisoning? After-wards, because we journos are terrible gossips – if we weren't we wouldn't be in this business – people talked about how they sometimes caught a rancid whiff on her breath. Sometimes her eyes were a little red. Her lipstick smudged. Yes, Maria Wiemann was an alcoholic.

On the way back, I thought about it. I'm no stranger to drink – especially in these last three months of my … sabbatical. The more you do it the better you get at it. From what I had heard Weimann was a high-functioning alcoholic. A pro. So how could she just get smashed like that?

I confirmed the disappearance of the man and the woman but there was no big conspiracy there. According to the daughter he had a wandering eye and was probably shacked up with a new woman. Her mother had an envious nature and refused to let him go. I was beginning to think the whole thing was nothing more than a coincidence – just one misfit following another into the void – but a few days at the archives confirmed I was on to something. Yes, this unremarkable little town was Germany's very own Bermuda Triangle.

After dinner I went out to find Atopia, the bar where Weimann had her last drink. "Turn right out of the *Pension* and take the second left. It's a few hundred metres down," said the goth. Her eyes were like dark pools in the dim light.

I stepped out into sharp evening air and set off at a brisk pace. The cello was playing again, its tempo faster now, more urgent. I was back on the trail of a story. The streetlamps cast everything in a greyish light. People scuttled by, ducking in and out of shops like ghosts. I passed one left turn and kept walking. The cello strokes faded behind me. Ahead, there was a major curve to the right before the road ended in darkness. A dead end marked by a looming dark mass.

Had I come too far? Missed the second left? I walked on, pulled towards the blackness. It was a massive unlit building. Probably the *Rathaus* – the town hall – a staple of every small German town. Still, there was something unnatural about its shadow-iness, the way light vanished at that point. As I got closer I fancied I could make out a thorny forest rising like a mysterious mountain in front of the building. The name of the town, *Teufelsberg* – Devil's Mountain in German – popped into my head. I stopped. There was an alley to my left. Was this the second turning? I ducked down it, escaping the terrible shadowy vision forming in front of me.

The alley widened into a road of row houses. There was no bar in sight. I took the next left, following the rule that *left, left, and left* gets you back to where you started. That was in the US though, where we had the grid system. It didn't work in these old European towns. I turned and turned getting further entangled in a web of little streets. Typical. This was what had landed me in trouble in the first place. Not knowing when to stop. What had led me from being Christian Finkel of *The New York Times*, reporting from Nigeria, Somalia and Afghanistan, to Christian Finkel whom no one would publish, lost and alone in a random German town.

My descent had started with a made-up quote here and there. You don't know what it's like in those places where people speak a hundred different dialects and even the translators get tongue-tied, where no one wants to talk and if they do it's to lead you on wild goose chases based on rumours, tales and fables, where you spend two days bumping along the desert to meet someone who doesn't turn up, or turns up three hours late looking to get paid. What was I supposed to do? Admit I couldn't file a story? The quotes had to be massaged. There was no other way. Plus, it *worked*. For a while anyway. I shouldn't have taken it further but I was enjoying my success, and the pressure to continue breaking stories grew. People recognised my name. At bars my gleaming image was reflected in the eyes of women, enchanted by my tales. Towards the end I was fabricating everything. The truth was elusive, impossible to get, didn't make any sense – and people wanted a story. It was only a matter of time before I got caught. *The Times* issued a full-page apology. *Your credibility is all you have as a journalist. Lose that and you're out of the game.* And I was out. My name smudged. Women turned away, repelled. I ignored calls from family and friends and decamped to Berlin, city of losers and wannabe artists. How was I going to get out of this mess? Was this how people disappeared here? They just got lost? My heart started to pound. I didn't want to die, to disappear into the oblivion in some small German town.

A deep low moan pierced my thoughts. Was it me? No, it was ... the cello. Rogue notes carried on the wind. I followed their direction, navigating my way through the crooked streets and piecing together the tune, until I emerged on the main road once more. I tramped back to the *Pension*, exhausted. The bar would have to wait until tomorrow.

The next morning everything seemed brighter. I peeled hardboiled eggs – their smooth white exteriors revealing wicked yellow insides – as I read the papers. I read the news every day. It was a habit I had kept up even in Berlin, where I was living off my savings drinking cheap beer, going to sex parties and nursing hangovers in my self-imposed exile. It stung seeing the names of my colleagues in print but reading the paper was the only thing that kept the days from blending into one another. It was a little bit of hope, proof that fresh stories and new developments emerged every day. That the world was still spinning and anything was possible.

I decided to give last night's directions another try. I turned right out of the *Pension*, passed the first left and there it was, a second left not soon after. I must have missed it in my excitement. The door of the bar was propped open by a couple of crates of beer. Inside it was dark and cigarette-smelling. A slot machine whirred and clinked in the corner fed by a thin sallow man.

"We're closed," came a voice from my left – a man loading beers into a fridge behind the bar.

"Hi. I just wanted to ask a few questions about my colleague Maria Weimann."

The bartender paused and turned. The slot machine whirred.

"You remember her?"

He nodded, once.

"What happened?"

"Drank too much, collapsed. They took her to hospital."

The slot machine emitted a jangle.

"Was she alone? Did she talk to anyone?"

"Just me."

"What did she talk to you about?"

"She told me what she wanted to drink."

I sighed as the slot machine fell silent. It was a typical German answer. Literal, direct. Despite being half-German myself it was a quality I loathed. Truth lay in the grey areas.

"And what was that?" I asked as the gambler dropped more coins into the machine.

"Vodka, gin, a few Jägermeisters – a mix."

The machine whirred.

"You kept serving her? Didn't think she'd had enough?"

"It's a bar. People order drinks. They get what they order."

Jangle. Jangle. Jangle.

"Yes, but an exceptionally high number of people have died of alcohol poisoning in this town and since this is one of only three bars—"

"Maybe it's time you left," said the man. It sounded like a warning. His eyes were like deep wells. Were he and the goth related? It wouldn't be unusual in a small town like this, then again, he was fair-haired and it was probably just the lighting in this dingy place that made his eyes resemble hers. I left, the sound of coins clinking behind me.

At the main road I turned left instead of heading back to the *Pension*. I needed to think, and to think I needed to walk. Plus, I wanted to see the *Rathaus*, or whatever it was, in daylight to banish the queasiness from last night. There was the curve to the right and straight ahead a redbrick building with a clock tower. Definitely the *Rathaus*. Behind it a mountain – or rather a hill – rose up. That accounted for the unusual shadowiness of the spot. In front of the building was a statue. I circled it: seven demons dancing atop a hill. Yes, all those horns and swinging tails could seem like thorny branches in the dark.

Each demon represented a deadly sin. Sloth was sprawled lazily on the slope of the hill, with Gluttony emptying a bottle into his mouth nearby. I thought of

Weimann and shuddered. Greed's fingers reached grabbingly into thin air. The figure of Lust was dominated by a grotesque erection. The man Weimann had written about in that first report had, according to his daughter, been lustful. Envy glanced at her companions through narrowed eyes. That was his wife. Wrath's eyes were made of copper, as was her raised sword. Vanity gazed into a black glass mirror and, rising above them all in the very centre, was Pride. My very own sin.

What was such a strange statue doing here in front of the town hall? *Teufelsberg.* Of course. It was a representation of the town's name. Devil's Mountain. For the first time, I wondered about the history of that name. I strolled on towards the *Rathaus.* Maybe someone there could tell me. It would be a colourful fact to throw into the article.

Inside, the *Rathaus* was disappointingly stale compared to its rich exterior. All signs for administrative buildings and long grey corridors. I turned down one at random, passing ticket-number dispensers and people milling in waiting areas, when I saw a sign saying *Bibliothek am Rathaus.* A library. Perfect. I followed the sign pushing through two sets of double doors before stepping into a dim space with towering bookcases. I paused and breathed in the musty air. It was disorienting, the way things morphed in this town.

I walked along a row of dusty books … Goethe, Schiller, Mann.

"The immortals," came a voice behind me. It was an

old man with pale skin, red hair and a wispy beard.

"Hi. I'm looking for information about the town's name ... Teufelsberg. It's unusual."

"Yes, yes," said the man. His eyes were like sunken black pebbles in the lined landscape of his face. I waited. Normally if you wait people will talk to fill the silence.

"It's a long story," he said finally and turned, his shoes tapping the stone floor as he walked further into the library. Did he expect me to follow? *Words, old man, use your words*, I thought as I trailed down the maze of aisles after him. He stopped and pulled a big leather-bound book from its shelf. *Das Komplette Geschiste vom Teufelsberg.* A Complete History of Teufelsberg. I took it. Its weight pressed my fingertips. The old man was right: it was a long story.

Tap, tap, tap.

"Wait, isn't there a short answer? I'm just visiting..." I said as the man disappeared around the end of a bookcase. I followed.

"I can't check this out – I'm not a member."

He turned down another aisle.

"I just need a few details for a story..."

The old man stopped and turned.

"To write a proper story you need to research. How else will you end up here with the immortals," said the man waving at the German greats on the shelf next to him. Somehow we had ended up back at the entrance. He was right of course. Rigorous research and fact-checking were exactly what I needed for my comeback.

"Take it. You can bring it back when you're finished," he said.

"What?"

The man's eyes were hard and determined. I shrugged and left with the book. What kind of a librarian was he? It was a wonder there were still any books left in there if that was how he ran the place. Must be losing his marbles.

I went back to the *Pension* to drop off the book. When I got there I sat in the armchair by the window. The cellist was playing again. Repeating that same tune with slight variations each time. I picked up the book; now was as good a time as any to do some background research. It wasn't as if there was anything further to be achieved today. Tomorrow I had an appointment with the local police station chief which would probably generate some new leads. I turned to the first page.

The hill, and surrounding lands – the area currently named Teufelsberg – is notable for its rich fertile soil. The Goths considered it a place of extraordinary natural power where they made human and animal sacrifices.

Talk about complete history. I skimmed over the next few pages detailing various excavations, belief systems and rituals until—

During the Christian era the area was named Teufelsberg being, as it was, a place associated with pagans and devil worshippers. Christians from the villages on the periphery of Teufelsberg were warned to stay away from the wild wooded area. Despite this an uncanny number of children and adults were recorded missing...

My neck prickled. Church records dating from the sixteenth century listed, with the same regularity as births, deaths and marriages, details of persons disappeared. The cellist switched to a higher register. I kept reading.

...resulting in the 1636-42 witch trials in which fifty-eight individuals were found guilty of luring people into the woods as offerings to the devil. Evidence included eyewitness accounts of bodies hanging from trees...

I thought about how, just yesterday, I had made that statue in front of the *Rathaus* out to be some kind of shadowy forest. Yes, it would be easy to do – imagine bodies hanging among the branches in a dark woodland. After all, people are prone to making up all sorts of things.

Other "evidence" from the witch trials included testimony from a farmer who claimed that the darker richer soil of Teufelsberg, compared to that of the surrounding farms, was a result of human blood and putrefaction. He obviously had an axe to grind over some nutrient deficit which caused his crops to fail in 1603, 1605, 1611, et al – but never affected the vegetation of Teufelsberg. I skipped forward.

It was only after the Second World War displaced millions, causing the biggest migration of people across Europe, that Teufelsberg became settled. Much of the woodland beneath the hill had been destroyed by fires caused by bombing, and the town was built on this wasteland, from the rubble of the war. The original settlers were said to have made a pact with the devil in order to live on his land. Upon making this deal the colour of their eyes turned the colour of the Teufelsberg soil to which they belonged. Their descendants are to this day still recognisable by their dark eyes...

I paused. The cellist was inserting extra phrases to his tune, making it longer, more complex. I had been pulled in. Suckered. This was no history book. It was folklore, presented as fact. I flipped to the cover. The author was Henri Faust. Was this a joke? I turned back to where I had left off. The book might have been a curious mix of fact and fiction, but it was a compelling read. Besides, something about the muted sunlight diffusing through the room and the cello's increasing momentum as it travelled further away from its original tune was hypnotic. I turned the page.

...and are said to continue to operate as tools of the devil by luring people to their deaths on this land. The native populations from the villages surrounding Teufelsberg always viewed the new town's inhabitants with suspicion, being, as they were, outsiders who arrived dark-eyed from the East with no clear history, place or...

Snap! I opened my eyes. I could still sense the vibration of the string, taut and high-pitched, before it snapped and silence descended. The clock glowed 02:38. Had the cellist been playing until now? Or had it been a dream? My ears pulsed in the stillness. I stood — the book slid to the floor with a thud – and crawled into bed, my eyelids heavy with sleep.

~~~

The police chief looked bewildered. His eyes and hair were the colour of mud, flecked with gold. The files on his desk were piled high like heaps of dead leaves that he had to wade through.

"What can I say? It's an anomaly. A coincidence." He shrugged. He had been repeating the same phrase in different ways throughout the interview. I got the feeling it was an explanation he repeated a lot, not just to me. I almost felt sorry for him. Almost. Another part of me wanted to punch him. He had given me nothing. Not a hint of a serial killer, a sect, or something sinister in the water. Just a shrug and a nod to the chaos of the universe.

As I walked back into town my eye caught a tall sharp figure hurrying down the street. I paused. Herr Koch! I hurried after him, turning down one street then another until I found myself on an empty road of row houses. There was nowhere he could have gone unless... Had he entered one of the houses? Was he selling knives in this neigh-bourhood? No, he was due to be in Nuremberg right now. It might not have been him but that figure, so distinct. I dug out my wallet and shuffled through a bunch of receipts and cards until I found his. I dialled his number and held my breath. This was ridiculous. What did I expect? Was he ducking behind a car, waiting to spring out like a Jack-in-the-Box? It rang and rang... Voicemail. I hung around for a bit waiting for him to come out of one of the houses. My fingers and toes started to turn numb. No one could discuss knives for this long. It was time to give up.

On my way back, I came across Atopia. Now was as good a time as any for a drink. The bartender raised his eyebrows at me when I walked in. I sat down and ordered a beer and a shot. Fuck him. Robert Johnson crackled through the speakers.

Standin' at the crossroad,
I tried to flag a ride,

Apart from me there was just one other guy nursing a beer and the gambler from yesterday, feeding coins into the machine.

Didn't nobody seem to know me,
Everybody pass me by

The story was dead. My Woodward and Bernstein moment gone. But... The machine whirred. If that was Herr Koch and he hadn't caught his train to Erfurt it was proof something odd was up. He could tell me why, what happened. He was the key to breaking this story. I tried calling him again.

Mmm, the sun goin' down, boy
Dark gon' catch me here

Voicemail again. The gambler dropped more coins into the machine. Idiot. I wanted to shake him. Didn't he know he was never going to win? He needed to do something else. *Jangle. Jangle. Jangle.* Shit. *I* needed to do something else. I was just like that guy. Delusional. I probably even imagined seeing Herr Koch. No, I wasn't about to become another lost soul in this small town. I needed to stop thinking I could win back my former glory and just get a nine-to-five. I didn't need to be Christian Finkel, journalist extraordinaire. I could be Average Joe. Normal. Anonymous. I downed the beer, threw down some coins and left.

I went straight to the train station. The cellist was

playing again, frantic and demented. Last night wasn't a dream. One of his strings really had snapped leaving his tune a little off. I walked past the blood-red marigolds as I entered the station – and remembered the book. All those fairy tales about the special Teufelsberg soil fertile with human putrefaction. I'd have to return it to the library before I left. I bought a ticket to Berlin for that very evening then went back to the *Pension* to fetch the book.

The *Rathaus* corridors were shushed with only the shuffle of papers and a few murmuring voices. People were leaving for the day. I wandered around searching for *Bibliothek am Rathaus*. Somehow, I couldn't find it. It was like a sign. I was going to disappear into the great blob of humanity, never to be remembered. I'd never make it into the library. How come I always lost my way in this damned town? I recalled a passage I had read last night.

The phenomenon of objects and buildings shifting and subsiding in Teufelsberg has been subject to much theorising. Architects and geologists are in agreement that the soil and rubble upon which the town was hastily built is still settling, accounting for a degree of movement and disorientation. Occultists argue that the town occupies a supernatural space which transmogrifies to tempt people into its net...

The fluorescent lights overhead started to flicker. Fuck this. I wasn't about to get trapped in some administrative building and miss my train. I'd leave the book at the *Pension*. I followed the *Ausgang* signs and made my way back.

I got to the station an hour early and paced up and down the platform thinking. That book. The way it described things shifting in this town felt true. And all that stuff about inhabitants having eyes as dark as the Teufelsberg soil? The goth at the *Pension*, the guy at the bar – even the librarian – had dark eyes. I strode over to the marigolds and peered between their petals: glistening black soil. My heartbeat quickened. No. Just because certain things in the book were on point didn't mean all that stuff about witches and the devil was. It was ludicrous. The book was just joining certain dots of reality, fabricating the space between. I couldn't do that. Not again. I was a journalist, I dealt in facts. It would be different if I had an actual source…

I tried Herr Koch again. It rang and rang. Voicemail. I tried him again and again. I was acting like a crazed stalker but I couldn't let go of the feeling I was onto something. The chance of the big break I needed to get out of this rut. The railroad started to rumble and the train to my new life of mediocrity approached. The phone rang. The train glided to a stop. The doors slid open. Shit. Answer your fucking phone. People got off. Voicemail. I hit redial. It rang. The doors started to close. He was going to pick up this time. This was going to work. I was too good for anything else. All those stories. Paedophilia in the Afghan Army. The Somalian Weapons Black Market. Corruption in the Nigerian Cabinet. The doors shuddered shut and the train chugged away. Voicemail. Fuck. What was I doing? It was over. My ears started ringing. I tried to breathe. Calm down. It wasn't a big deal. What difference did it make if I was down and out in Berlin or here? I would just get another ticket for tomorrow. That's when I noticed it. The phone flashing. The ringing wasn't in my head – someone was calling. Herr Koch. I answered.

"Herr Koch. Christian Finkel here. I'm sorry, I just realised my phone mistakenly dialled—"

"Actually, I thought you might still be in Teufelsberg and were calling about that drink," said Herr Koch.

"What? You're here?"

~~~

Herr Koch looked different. His cheeks were fuller, flushed. He welcomed me into a row house on the road where I had lost him the other day. It smelt of warm bread and cakes. My stomach rumbled. When had I last eaten? I smiled as Herr Koch introduced me to Marta, a plump woman in a white apron embroidered with purple flowers, Katrin, a doll-like girl, and Kilian, a polite serious boy. I tried to make sense of this picture.

In the living room Marta poured tea into porcelain cups and served cake on doily napkins. This wasn't my idea of a drink but I was glad for the food. In all this obsessing over the story I had neglected to eat. Had Herr Koch moved to Teufelsberg with his family? But didn't his children have different names? I wracked my brain trying to remember.

Katrin sang a song then curtsied. Kilian recited a Goethe poem. I pretended to be charmed. They weren't acting like normal children. They had dark eyes like their mother. Herr Koch's grey eyes, or any of his features, were nowhere to be seen. They were not his children. Marta brought in some cookies then slices of freshly baked bread with butter and honey. I watched Herr Koch eat. No wonder he seemed fuller. Finally the kids went off to play and Marta brought us two *Weissen* beers along with some pretzels and "left us men to it".

"So, the last time I saw you, at the station..." I started.

"Oh yes, that's where I met Marta. It started as a chat but by the time the train came I knew I wasn't ready to leave."

"But what about your job? Your—" I lowered my voice to a whisper "—wife, children."

Herr Koch crammed some pretzels into his mouth.

"All of that just wasn't working out. With Marta I feel like I've finally found what I have been looking for..."

By the time I stepped out into the cold evening air I was reeling. My stomach churned with cake and pretzels. Thank God I had managed to get out of the roast dinner Marta had been insisting I stay for. I needed to gather my thoughts. I started walking.

The facts, Finkel. Stick to the facts.

Herr Koch, who was supposed catch a train to Erfurt, had been tempted to stay in Teufelsberg by Marta, a well-off widow. Her eyes were the same colour as the soil beneath the marigolds. Teufelsberg soil. Herr Koch was now engulfed in perfect family bliss. I recalled the brief conversation we had had on the train here. It was as if he had been tempted by his deepest need: his desire for a comfortable home and family life. Was this all a coincidence or proof that Teufelsberg's inhabitants really were operating as tools of the...? I stopped myself. Facts. Right. I recalled a passage from the book.

In 1961 the US National Security Agency (NSA) built a field station atop the hill to listen in on Soviet and East German military communications. The station closed after just one year due to an exceptional level of false alarms causing high levels of anxiety and panic among the soldiers stationed there. Many of them had breakdowns or went AWOL. The few available documents from the station do indeed support the theory that the soldiers were suffering from stress. Many of them claimed that they were not in fact picking up military signals but tuning into the thoughts of the people who lived below the hill...

Was this land and the folk who belonged to it able to pick up on people's thoughts, morphing in order to feed their desires and lure them into darkness? The ground felt as if it was pulsing, undulating beneath my feet – or maybe it was my own pulse, my excitement at finally piecing together a story. The problem was, I needed proof. Facts. Not only because I needed to re-establish my integrity as a journalist but because a story like this, that involved supernatural elements, would need to be substantiated. But that very word – *supernatural* – meant something that went beyond the natural world, beyond what could be touched, seen, proven.

I walked around town getting lost in its labyrinthine streets, turning the problem round in my head. There had to be a way. I needed to verify. Investigate. I was a great journalist. I was Christian Finkel of the *NYT*. If anyone could do it, it was me.

I stopped at Atopia to talk to the gambler. His bones jutted beneath his saggy pale skin. He reeked of piss. How long had he been sitting here?

"Excuse me, could I ask you a few questions?"

He didn't blink. His eyes were fixated on the machine. If he wasn't careful he was going to die on that stool. I moved on.

The more I walked the more I saw it. This town was filled with crazed people, spiralling in a *Teufelskreis* – a devil's cycle, unable to escape. I took notes. Peered into people's eyes to see what colour they were, stopped them on the street to get interviews, quotes. I banged on the cellist's door. His tune was becoming desperate, obsessed. His silhouette, like a deranged puppet in the window, never paused. He never stopped to answer the door. One by one the rest of his strings snapped. Then silence. The gambler disappeared. This town was eating up people. Somebody had to do something about it. Somebody had to save them. Herr Koch was getting fatter. We met sometimes. I told him he needed to leave. He told me I needed to leave. We stayed. He couldn't get up from his armchair. I couldn't stop walking, thinking.

The heels of my shoes were wearing out, my clothes became looser. I was going to make it into that library. I was going to go down in history. Once I was done with this story everyone would want it. *The Guardian, The Times*... there would be a bidding war, a book deal, a Pulitzer. I was going to cause a sensation, rock the foundations of modern thought, smash rationalism.

LIRPALOOF ISLAND

Garry Kilworth

When I was a mere operative in OCC, working on an island in the Pacific Ocean, the company laid a communications cable between Japan and Hong Kong under the South China Sea. A unit containing a microphone was installed every hundred miles along the cable. These units were there to detect any interference with the cable, such as deep-sea fishermen accidentally damaging our equipment. However, we were astonished to discover that the microphones were picking up the sounds of WW2 sea battles between Japan and the Allies; battles apparently recorded by deep cold-water currents that acted in the same way as magnetic tapes. I tell you about this astonishing phenomenon in order to prepare you for the following story, which may on the surface appear fantastic, but which I assure you is a true account of one of those strange warps or kinks in the laws of the universe which we believe to be immutable.

~~~

There's always a fall guy in any office. A gullible member of staff: the brunt of all the jokes. At the time all this took place, I was the CEO for the Overseas

Communications Company, a firm which supplies and runs the telecommunications systems for small island groups which did not have the technological ability to establish and operate their own telephone and telex systems. Now, getting back to fall guys, the man who had that role in our Head Office was William Mcleod. The first thing our Chairman, Abe Hamber, said when Bill joined the company was, "I hope you haven't got your head in the clouds, Bill, because we need sharp minds around here." We all laughed at that, Abe being the boss.

Shortly before April the first came around I got the call from Abe and went to his office, to find Clara there already. Clara was the Vice Chair of the company, so I knew this was going to be a hush-hush meeting. I was on my guard because Abe was famous throughout the business world for his April Fool jokes.

His most famous joke, a legend now, was when he had one of our telephone engineers go into Head Office the night before the first to take the phones apart. The engineer rewired the number buttons so that if someone pressed, say, 0202 348732 they would actually be dialling 6868 573418 or whatever. Then the next morning Abe watched as chaos ensued amongst his bewildered staff. It all went as he had planned until old Joe Keppling – who could never take chaos without getting over-stressed – Joe had a heart attack and the people who were dialling 999 were getting nowhere until some bright spark thought to use a mobile

"In a few days' time," Abe said to the two of us,

"it'll be the first of April."

I nodded and smiled. "What have you got up your sleeve this year?"

He leaned forward, elbows on his huge oak desktop.

"Elaborate ain't the word for it," he said, grinning.

Clara said, "I hope it's not too cruel."

"Don't be a party pooper, Clara," replied Abe. "He'll come to no harm. In fact he might enjoy it, once he knows."

"So," I said, surprised. "Just one victim?"

"Bill Mcleod. He's the only one who would fall for it. Any of the others would see through it. It's a real doozie, this one."

"So tell," I said.

Abe chuckled to himself for a few moments, then told us: "I'm sending Mcleod to Lirpaloof Island. The station there seems to have got itself in an operational mess. If Mcleod does a good job I'll tell him, there might be a promotion in the offing."

"Lurpa what?" I said. "Where the hell is that?"

"In some ocean somewhere," cried Abe, nodding at Clara who had cast her eyes to heaven. "Ha! Ha! He'll have a whale of a time drinking piña coladas and sunning himself on the sands. Of course—" he winked at us "—there's a few dangerous creatures there. Snakes and scorpions, that kind of thing. But the beach parties will make up for that – barbecues under the palms – and the girls. Yes, I know Clara, but I'm sorry this is no time to spoil a good joke with PC. The girls there are buxom and willing, Polynesians naturally, or similar dusky maiden types. Can you imagine Bill Mcleod, glasses slipping down that narrow nose of his in a sweaty climate, getting down and dirty with a hula girl? I have to wonder if the guy has ever had a hard on. Yes, yes, all right Clara, I'll shut up. Well Jack, waddya think?"

"I still don't understand," I said, feeling uncomfortable under Clara's hard stare. "Where's the joke in sending him to an island in the sun?"

Abe snorted. "Shall I send you instead, Jack?"

Clara let out a huge sigh. "Oh for fuck's sake, Jack, Lirpaloof is April Fool backwards. There's no such island. It's a fiction."

"Brilliant, eh?" cried Abe, slapping the desktop with a heavy palm. "My PA will fix him an electronic air ticket which will take him to Auckland and on arrival there he's expected to book his own flight to Lirpaloof Island using Turtle Airways—" he winked again "—a small airline dealing with offshore destinations."

"Won't Mcleod see through this before he even gets on the long-haul flight? Clara did."

"But you didn't," Abe pointed out, "and the man is not as bright as we hoped, we know that now. In fact he's pretty short on initiative. I should have sacked him a month after he arrived, but hell, he's fun to have around. Someone's got to take the flak, otherwise it might be me."

I said, "I don't think anyone would dare..."

"No, neither do I—" cut in Abe "—I'm just spouting. Anyway, what do you think? Think the rest of the staff will have a laugh?"

I nodded enthusiastically, Clara less so. Abe was Abe and anything we said would have no effect on deterring him. This hoax would go ahead and neither Clara nor me would have the courage to tell Bill Mcleod what the company Chairman was up to. I persuaded myself it might even be fun for the victim. After all, he was going to get a free flight to New Zealand and back, and would probably get a nice hotel, meal and drinks on expenses while he was there.

Abe was going to tell Mcleod two hours before his flight that he needed to go immediately to the island. It was an emergency. This would give him no time to ponder over the destination. Abe was going to hand him sealed instructions on what to do and when. Even if he unravelled the name on the flight over, I was convinced Bill would not dare to open the envelope until he arrived in Auckland. He was a man trapped by his character. He took the office jokes against him solemnly, but without complaint. It was as if he knew his role in life and had accepted it long ago. At school he must have been bullied mercilessly. At least in the office he was held somewhat in affection.

And so the day came. He was called to Abe's office and given strict, hasty instructions. Abe personally imposed the importance of the mission on him, and Abe's PA and Human Resources swiftly arranged the paperwork needed. The firm's car chauffeured him to his flat to collect his passport and pack a small bag. I accompanied him to his flat and the airport, talking to him the whole time about everything and nothing, to keep his mind occupied. Poor Mcleod was whirled this way and that in order to get him on that flight to Auckland. Indeed, he seemed delighted with all the attention, which made me feel bad on seeing the recrimination in Clara's eyes. I don't think he had time to even consider decoding the name of the place to which he had been sent or to contemplate the nature of his destination.

The morning after his departure I hurried to Head Office and went straight to Abe Hamber. When I knocked and entered, he was reading something on his laptop. I sat down without being asked. His seniority was only marginally above my own.

"Fuck!" he said, looking up at me with a puzzled expression. "Email from Mcleod: *I have lost envelope containing instructions —*"

"He would do that," I said, nodding. "He loses everything."

"*—however, will proceed to Lirpaloof to ascertain problems and hopefully to solve them. Will report back once I have arrived. W Mcleod.*"

"Proceeding? But is there a real Lirpaloof?"

Abe shook his head. "I've already made several calls, to the Foreign Office, to the British Library and even the Royal Geographical Society. There is no and never has been a Lirpaloof Island."

"You think the Kiwis are taking the piss out of him too, then?"

"Maybe. Or maybe Mcleod is cleverer than we think – what about if he's turning the whole joke on us?"

"It wouldn't be in character, Abe. You know what he's like. He absorbs the fun poked at him. He just gives you that watery smile and says, 'You got me there, fellah.' That's all he ever does. I've never known him to take umbrage or say anything else. He's a sponge and sponges don't turn jokes on the jokers. No, especially one as elaborate and costly as this one. Not Mcleod. No way."

"You're right. He's too wet. But you would have thought by now he'd have worked out the back-to-front name?"

"Abe," I said, "there's an Easter Island. There's a Christmas Island. The Whitsundays. Hawaii was once called the Sandwich Islands. Captain Cook even named a town 1770 when he'd run out of names. Maybe Mcleod really believes there's an April Fool Island, the name of which was reversed for the sake of humour?"

At that moment Clara entered the office with an envelope in her hand.

"He did leave it behind," she said. "His landlady brought it in."

"His sealed instructions," Abe said. "The note that would have told him it was all an April Fool's joke."

"Still," I said, "he could have worked it out anyway." I paused, shook my head and added, "but not to call in and say, 'You got me there, sir!'."

Clara said, "He might be in trouble. Perhaps his state of mind? You know? You must make enquiries, Abe."

Abe took her seriously. He made calls to the long-haul airline, to Auckland Airport authorities, to the New Zealand police, the hospitals and to Immigration Services. No one knew where this W Mcleod was. He had indeed entered the country but no one was sure where he'd gone after he left the airport and whether he was still on New Zealand soil. An enquiry had now been set up and any member or members of staff responsible for dereliction of duty would be reprimanded. New Zealand took its administrative duties seriously.

Everyone, it seemed, was taking things seriously but no one was coming up with answers.

~~~

A month later we received a call from a New Zealand fisherman. He had netted a bottle containing a message. The sender had indicated that the finder should contact Sir Abraham Hamber of the Overseas Communications Company, London. However, before the fisherman would read it to us over the telephone he wanted assurance that there would be a reward, since the call was costing him "an orm and a lig". Kiwis do this funny thing with their vowels, exchanging the phonetics, so that a "e" becomes an "i" and "pen" becomes "pin" and the "i" becomes a "u" and you get "fush and chups". Not easy for a Brit to follow, especially taking it down on a keyboard as it's spoken.

The fisherman was told the amount would be more than adequate. I typed the letter with difficulty on Abe's computer as it was read to us in a twangy Kiwi accent.

Dear Sir Abraham,

I am not quite sure why I've been sent to Lirpaloof, but I would appreciate it, sir, if you could manage to arrange for me to leave as soon as possible. On arrival at Auckland Airport I enquired about Turtle Airways. No one had heard of it. So, using my initiative I took a taxi to the nearest yacht marina and asked everyone I met if they knew how to get to Lirpaloof Island. I wasn't successful until around midnight when a man stepped out of the shadows – I remember his hair was as white as salt and his skin like tree bark – and he said he would take me to there. He had amongst his tattoos one of an island group which covered his chest. He pointed to it, saying, "This is the archipelago, the atoll, my friend. This one at the bottom, is the island you need." I recall climbing into his canoe with some reservations, but by this time I was desperate and also exhausted with jet lag. I fell asleep in the bottom of the pahi.

I next really only became fully conscious of my surroundings on finding myself on the beach of this godforsaken place. I thought at first to acquaint myself with the procedures used in the local station, but have so far been unable to locate anything that resembles a communications centre. Also, conditions are not what I expected, even though you warned me of certain dangers. There are various creatures on this island to be avoided. Indeed, even the locals are less than friendly and treat me as an interloper. They are of a rather savage nature and if it is not unacceptable to say so, of a primitive mind. There are ugly pagan rituals the details of which I will not go into here, but I honestly believe they practise bestial sacrifice, perhaps even worse.

Please, sir, find a way to get a loyal and faithful employee passage away from here, I beg you. I am sleeping rough on the beach and finding food where it drops from the trees. The local fishermen ignore my pleas for transport and there is no ferry. I am at a loss to know where to turn to next.

Yours sincerely,

W Mcleod

PS. Of one thing I am absolutely certain. This is Lirpaloof Island. The name is up on the shack that serves as a store and whenever I ask a local, he or she always confirms the fact. I am happy to report, sir, that I carried out the first part of my instructions, to reach my destination, though without one of our comcens I am unable to perform the rest of my duties.

"We have to get him home," whispered Clara. "The poor boy."

"Get him home? Get him home? For fuck's sake, Clara," I cried, "he's on a fictitious island!"

Abe said, "We have to send someone else, someone with a few brains, to find him and bring him back."

"Does no one listen to me?" I said. "He's told us where he is and it doesn't exist. Abe has confirmed that with every living authority."

I knew with both Clara and Abe that I was dealing with unimaginative people. They were pragmatists who dealt in scientific fact, but I had to persuade them that what we were dealing with here was the preternatural world. It was not going to be easy.

"Look," I began, "you have to develop a little imaginative elasticity. It may be hard to accept standing here in this office, but space, time and dimensions are not set in stone. There are those scientists who truly believe in time travel. There are those who believe in the flexibility of space. And more relevant to our problem, there are those who believe in more than three dimensions. Abe, Clara, have you ever heard of the theory of parallel worlds, where the earth that we live on is only one of many similar earths?"

"Heard of it," replied Abe, grudgingly. "Films and stories."

"Well, I believe that what's happened here is that Bill Mcleod has slipped into another dimension."

"How would he manage to do that?" asked Clara. "Accepting that there is such a place."

"Because he really believes that Lirpaloof exists. He's been told so by the chairman of the company he works for, a man he looks up to as a god. He's found his way to Lirpaloof because he's convinced it's there, just as those who believe you get to Heaven if you have faith in its existence probably get there too."

Abe said, "Shit, this is too far-fetched for me, Jack."

"Look," I replied, sighing deeply, "I know it sounds unbelievable, but I'm simply trying to cover all bases here. Mcleod has been missing for weeks now, and all we have is a bottle with a message in it. We can still keep exploring the idea that he's been stranded on a real island that the locals have decided to call Lirpaloof, but probably has another name on the charts—"

"I really do like that idea," murmured Abe, firmly.

"—but we can also open our minds to the

possibility—" I held up my hands "—the very remote possibility, that we're dealing with the otherworldly here. You know I spent several years in the Pacific as the manager of one of our comcens—"

"Kula Mahi Islands," said Clara. "You came home a little strange from that place, Jack."

"—well, those isolated volcanic islands do things to your heart and your head. They retain some of the mystical elements of their early histories. There are tremendous electric storms that come sweeping in out of the sea, the like of which we never see in this safe land of ours. The scenery is uncanny: high escarpments with weird shapes to them which do eerie things with the sound of the wind. Deep impenetrable jungled interiors where men live without contact with the modern world. The retention of ancient rituals, even though the islanders may follow a modern religion on the surface."

I realised I was in danger of sounding like an ex-colonial here and I could see Clara was beginning to purse her lips.

"Oh, I'm not saying all the Pacific islands are like this, just one or two forgotten ones, away from the shipping lanes, out in the blue isolated darkness of the largest ocean on the earth. I just know that on the Kula Mahis I learned to let go of reality once in a while, to open myself to experience the numinous of an ancient landscape, and the barely concealed beliefs of its inhabitants. It was actually enlightening, rather than upsetting. I came home feeling I had expanded my mind and my spirit."

"All this is very well," broke in Abe and I knew I hadn't changed his scepticism one jot, "but what about the bottle with the message in it. Did it float across dimensions? How does it get from one world to another? Tell me that, Merlin."

"Well, of course I can't give you a definite answer, Abe. But what I will say, that if there is a passage between dimensions, between parallel worlds, it would be on an open stretch of water with no land in sight and no sign of the now. Just the winds, the sea and the sky. Eddies, tides, deep water currents, the ocean swells, they do strange things and find and reach unusual places. They find hidden caves and unknown shoals. They reach the depths of our world, places which have never been seen by the eyes of Man. They enter the narrowest cracks, the tightest fissures in the skull of the earth. They curl, they rip, they tear away the landscape to reveal lost wonders. And if there is a way to cross time and space, people, it's out on those watery wastes, unseen by you or me. A bottle drifting aimlessly, caught and carried by currents and waves? I would say that might be the way to cross from one parallel world to another."

"We need to send someone to investigate," stated Abe, firmly. "Someone who doesn't know I invented the name of the island. If Mcleod can get there then maybe someone else can too. Two heads may be able to find a way off that place, where one is left dithering, especially as that one head is stuck on the shoulders of Bill Mcleod."

"Well it can't be me or Clara because we are two

people who believe that the island is fictitious. Can I suggest it should be someone who is open to the idea of the paranormal? You don't need to tell them that there's the possibility the island doesn't exist. Just send them out with unencumbered information, but with a mind able to accept the fantastical as well as the reality of this world or any other."

"Bates," said Clara, quickly.

"Bates?" Abe and I echoed in unison and I added, "Who's he?"

"She. Alison Bates. She works in the mailroom."

Abe frowned. "How do you know she believes in – what is it? The supernatural?"

Clara looked a little defiant. "Because we were once an item."

"Oh," I said, "so you know her pretty well."

"Very well. She'll jump at the chance of an adventure that's paid for by the firm."

Abe wasn't thoroughly convinced by the idea but as he said later, what else was there? Mcleod was festering on some hostile landscape, probably nearing starvation or being treated like an animal by unfriendly locals and we had no real plan for getting him back. Indeed, he was a poor lost soul unless we could find some way to reach him, whether the island was real or fabricated.

Abe still believed that the island was real and some local sailor had taken advantage of Bill and dumped him on a place with a name close enough to Lirpaloof to fool his passenger. It would take a lot to stretch the mind of Abe Hamber, Chairman of the Overseas

Communications Corporation, a man who dealt solely in paperwork and board meetings. Abe wasn't even a comms man. He hadn't come up from operations like Clara and me. He was one of those businessmen who move from company to company, acutely aware of finances, personnel and global planning, but no engineer or communications operator.

Clara was right about Alison Bates though. She was tremendously enthusiastic about the project we'd given her. She was a small woman, around twenty-five, with dark hair and dark flashing eyes. Not once during the telling of the tale did she look as if she was going to laugh at us. Her expression was intent. She asked some serious and pertinent questions after the briefing, then told us she would bring William Mcleod back or die trying.

"I'll bring your boy home," said Alison, as I drove her to the airport. "Don't you worry for second, sir."

Foolishly, I believed her.

~~~

We heard nothing for several more weeks, then we received the second bottle message from Bill Mcleod. The "Dear Sir Abraham" had been thrown to the winds. It seemed we had crossed William's anger threshold at last.

Listen, you bastards at home, safe in your bloody comfortable offices in the middle of London. Alison Bates arrived on the island just a week ago. Unlike me, soft-treading Mcleod, she waded into the tribal elders and made demands. Last night they sacrificed her, live and naked, to some rock they worship. Her intestines were hung on an ancient tree and they dangle over a river. Fish with razor teeth leap out of the water to snap mouthfuls of her blood-dripping colon. Her torso was eventually thrown to some huge reptiles. Oh, and they hung her head on a string outside the village so that it would attract the flies and keep them from the huts. For fuck's sake get your fingers out and get me out of this hell hole. I know they're coming for me next. I have built a palm hut on the beach and I hear them outside, whispering and laughing. I'm terrified. What happened to Alison is nothing to what they'll do to me. Women are despatched quickly because they are held in some reverence. Men are toyed with just as cats play with mice. I've seen them take three days over killing a marooned sailor, whose screams seemed to delight the audience as they skinned him alive with scallop shells, and then fried his genitals while still attached to his body. There is no grave for the victims. Any pieces of their body left over is tossed to those giant lizards I told you about They have such strong jaws, they can crush and even swallow bones – skull, pelvis and everything else.

GET ME OFF THIS ISLAND, YOU ARSEHOLES!

PS. I've run out of the paper I brought with me in my briefcase now and the ink in my ballpoint pen is hardening. This is my last message. Tell Louise I love her desperately and will always love her. She is the brightest star in the firmament of my life. WM.

We were devastated of course. One of the worst aspects of it was, we had no idea who Louise was or where to find her. We went through Bill's desk drawers but there were no clues there. His landlady was not helpful, saying she had never heard of a

Louise and that Mr Mcleod's letters were all bills or junk mail. No one tried to contact the company, as might be expected when someone goes missing, and Bill's only surviving relative, an Aunt Rosimund, had not heard from him since he sent her a thankyou note for a birthday present when he was ten years of age. After that time, she said, she got no thanks and so stopped sending gifts altogether.

~~~

Poor Alison too! Clara wept for several hours and Abe kept repeating, "I'm never going to do another April Fool's joke. Never." For my part, I couldn't get the picture of that lovely energetic young woman as fierce in her determination to find and bring home Bill Mcleod mirrored Stanley's quest for Livingstone.

"She was such a gutsy girl," I said.

A tearstained Clara retorted, "I don't think that's appropriate, do you, considering what they did to her." And I realised what I'd said and apologised to everyone in the room.

~~~

Abe went burning into action now and mobilised politicians, the military and life-saving services. He did not mention that the island might be fictional. He merely reported Bill missing and said that the young man had gone in search of a place which was not on any known map and had not been heard from since. We said Bill was supposed to be somewhere in the region of Tasmanian Sea. Ships, boats, yachts and other seafaring vessels were sent messages and asked to be on the look-out for any suspicious craft or uncharted atoll. Abe even hired aircraft to scour the area, but not only did they find no Lirpaloof archipelago, they found no island whatsoever. Bill Mcleod was lost on a small kink in time and space.

After six months the whole episode was put on the archive shelves of Head Office, with a note to say that no OCC employee should ever be sent to a foreign station alone. Of course rumours circulated amongst the staff. One bad-taste joker wrote on the toilet wall "OCCult" which I was glad was in the Men's and out of Clara's view.

Just a week after the Bill Mcleod incident was shelved we received the final letter in a bottle, this time apparently from the Lirpaloof elders.

Ew terger ot mrofni uoy taht ruoy tnavres doelcM W saw dellik dna netae yb a odomok nogard. Lirpaloof Licnuoc.

DEATH AND THE WEAVER

Lou Morgan

The map was lying. There was no other explanation for it. She had definitely taken the third exit at the Quimper roundabout and, frankly, there was nowhere else she could have gone wrong. Sarah spread the creases of the map as flat as she could across the steering wheel and hunched forward, peering into the gloom. She should have listened to the lawyer.

It wasn't like she was lost. You couldn't get lost when you were going back to somewhere, could you? Especially if it was somewhere you'd spent every summer when you were a child.

Even if you hadn't actually been back there in more years than you wanted to remember, and it looked like there wasn't just a new road, but an entire new town in between you and where you were trying to go.

Sarah pulled the car over to the side of the road and rumpled the map into a ball, tossing it into the passenger seat with the empty sandwich packet and the folder of paperwork the lawyer had handed her – right before he suggested she might want to check into a hotel for the night rather than make the drive up to Locronan tonight.

"The weather changes fast up there in the autumn – perhaps you aren't familiar with it if you know it in the summer. You will remember the weather, yes?"

She hadn't. The weather, much like the road, was something she'd managed to forget in the years between visits. How the cloud swept down from nowhere, wrapping around the hills and smothering the little town in a clammy grey blanket. How the rain could manage to be horizontal, and somehow wetter than rain anywhere else. And now she was sitting in the middle of it. In the dark. With a map that was printed in 1985, which had what looked like a smear of mustard across one of the major roads. Now it was going dark and of course there were no streetlights.

She smacked both her hands on the steering wheel in frustration.

She should *definitely* have listened to the lawyer.

~~~

The letter had come out of the blue. It had taken seven phone calls and most of a bottle of wine to work out that following the sudden death of some particularly obscure relative, she was now the proud owner of a slightly dilapidated house in Cornouaille. She'd sat back in her chair and emptied the rest of the bottle of wine into her glass.

"Tell me what I should do," she'd asked the empty room. It didn't answer.

In the end, it was her agent's idea that she move out to the house for a while. She could hear him rolling his eyes on the other end of the phone. "You're behind with your pieces, and the gallery's fine for now.

Maybe the change of scene will do you good. New air. New colours. New … something?"

"Hint taken."

"I'm just saying."

"You're saying the gallery's pissed off."

"You've asked them to push back the show, Sarah. Twice. They don't like that."

"You mean you don't like it."

"I mean if you don't show, none of us get paid. So, no. I don't like it."

"Fine." She sounded more petulant than she'd meant to.

"You're going to give me the 'blocked' speech again, aren't you?"

"And you're going to give me the 'weavers don't get blocked' speech again in return, aren't you?"

"So we've shorthanded it. Wonderful. Look, I've got to run to a meeting. You know: with one of my clients who actually pays my bills?"

"You're a bottomless well of sympathy."

"Why I'm an agent and not an artist, petal," he said with a laugh and hung up. Sarah smiled and dropped her phone back onto the table, flipping through the photos the lawyer had sent. She remembered the house, dimly. It stood on the edge of the square in the oldest part of town, tall and narrow and with moss growing out of the cracks in the granite blocks. In her memory of it, the windows were open to the sunshine. Cheerful blue-painted window boxes were stuffed with yellow flowers, and an old-fashioned glass and wrought iron lantern (the closest thing the square had to streetlights) swung from the end of an arm bolted to the stone. It had cast flickering shadows on the walls of the bedroom she slept in whenever they stayed there, as they had for weeks every summer. At the time, she had never really thought of the house they spent all that time in as belonging to someone, being something anybody could own. All that mattered was that it meant "family". Or it had, anyway. Now it belonged to her. Just her. The name in the lawyer's letter was unfamiliar: a cousin of some kind, and it was jarring, somehow, to think that time had moved on there just as it had everywhere else.

She would sell the house. It was the sensible thing to do, looking at the photos. It was damp. Old, not the kind of place she had the time – or energy for. And then she saw the loom. It was standing in the middle of the single room that made up the ground floor of the house, shrouded in cobwebs. No-one had touched it for years, by the look of it. No-one, not since her father, who had taught her how to weave on it the summer it had rained.

So there she was, leaning over her steering wheel and swearing at the rain, with a hired car full of boxes and a tatty little transit van containing the rest of her worldly goods following a day behind. She should have remembered the rain. "Well, fine," she said to the empty sandwich packet and the crumpled map … and the scattering of apple cores, crisp packets and biscuit wrappers that littered the footwell next to her. "Fine, fine, fine." She started the engine again.

She was almost sure she was back on the right track

(and almost as sure that one of the headlights was about to give up the ghost) when she heard the sound of another engine coming up fast behind her. Well. fastish. It had sounded like it was coming up quickly but there was no sign of anything in the rear-view mirror. No headlights, at least – nothing. Not until there was a sudden whoosh of water into the side of her car, rocking it gently as a small, battered van belted past her and disappeared off up the road.

Without stopping to think about it, Sarah put her foot down and shot off into the darkness after the rapidly fading rear lights.

~~~

She lost the van pretty quickly: whoever the driver was, it was clear that he or she was, amongst other things, certifiable, throwing the van into corners and waiting until the very last possible second to brake. However hard she tried to keep up, hoping it would lead her to somewhere she recognised (or could at least find on the map), she never seemed to get any closer, and after a little while even the glow of the rear lights was lost to the darkness. Not that it mattered, because as the last glimmer of red faded into nothing, a white sign appeared at the side of the road.

Bienvenue à Locronan.

The little car park was nothing more than a cleared field, more mud than it was grass. Another thing she'd forgotten: no cars in the square. It would make unloading the van fun. It hadn't been important when she was a kid. When they arrived at the start of the summer, she had always run on ahead past the hotels and the restaurants and the tourist shops, down the road all the way to the town square; leaving her father to trail behind with the bags. The square had opened up before her, with its cobbles and its church and its wishing well and the rickety wooden stage where the artists sold portraits; just as it did now, in the rain. And there, almost directly across from her and next to the church, was the house.

The smell wrapped around her when she opened the door. Old stone and dust and pockets of damp. And wood and wool, because there was the loom, waiting for her. The light from the streetlamp outside, the only light, poured in through the open door and cast long shadows behind the wooden beams of the frame. There was still cloth on it, still thread in the shuttle which rested on the side as though it had only been set down for a moment. Her fingers left clean stripes in the velvety dust that had settled on the wood.

There was a candle half-melted onto the granite of the windowsill. Next to it was a box of matches. The cardboard felt slightly damp to the touch, but the first match that Sarah struck caught and the little candle at least gave her enough light to close the door, find a chair and collapse into it a little after midnight.

~~~

"Bernez? It would be nice if I still had a bedroom floor left by the time you're done." Sarah leaned round the top of the tightly spiralled stone stairs and handed a mug of coffee to her neighbour, who was busy yanking handfuls of wiring out from under the boards on the first floor. He shook his head at her as he took the mug.

"A few holes in the floor, or electricity? It's up to you, of course."

"You win." She gave him her best smile, and he grunted back at her. It was as good a response as she was likely to get. The two months since she'd moved in had taught her as much. Bernez, a heavily-built man in his late fifties, lived in one of the houses behind the square and thought of himself as a jack-of-all-trades. Builder, electrician, plumber, decorator; expert on politics, economics and anything else which happened to catch his eye. He was, however, kind and friendly and had gone out of his way to look after her since she'd arrived. It was Bernez who had got the ancient gas cooker in the kitchen working, Bernez who had checked the chimneys and shown her how to build and light a fire that stayed lit and didn't smoke her out of the house; Bernez who had evicted the family of rats from the bathroom and who had tracked down a shower which fitted in the impossibly small space for it and which actually ran hot. All she had to do in return was keep the coffee coming and ignore the fact that everything she owned smelled like an ashtray.

She was settling in better than she'd expected to. It had only taken a day or two to arrange her belongings in the house, and Bernez had turned up on her doorstep the morning after she'd arrived, tool bag in his hand, to offer his services. It made him feel useful, he said. Bad health had forced him to retire, selling his business in the process. "The stress. My heart," he'd said, gesturing to his chest with a hand like a bear's paw. Sarah had managed not to comment on the cigarette between his fingers at the time, but only just. She liked Bernez. She still hadn't *quite* forgiven him for the hangover from the terrifyingly strong drink he called "flip", and which he'd given her at the welcome party he'd thrown for her, but she liked him.

While Bernez worked on the electrics, the plumbing and the everything-else, she'd worked on the loom. It wasn't in too bad a state, considering, and a couple of days' attention with a hammer, a screwdriver and some sandpaper put it in pretty good shape. When she blew the dust off the cloth, it was a shock to see the familiar pattern in front of her. The same one she'd learned with her father. It was the same cloth. No-one had ever finished it. They had simply left it, waiting for her to come back. And now she had.

When her agent Jonny finally managed to get hold of her, he thought finishing it for the show was the best idea she'd ever had. Another thing Sarah had discovered on her first day in the house was that the thick stone walls made it almost impossible to get a mobile signal – in fact, to get one she had to walk back through the square and up the hill to the row of little cottages perched like rotten teeth at the top. And even then, it wasn't reliable.

The place was perfect.

She was closing the shutters one evening when she heard the engine again. That same noise: halfway between an angry hairdryer and a very, very, small chainsaw. Pulled up on the other side of the square was a battered little 2CV van, its engine hiccupping in the dusk. There was the sound of hammering, and a pair of legs appeared from underneath it as its owner rolled himself out across the cobbles. He stood up, trying to wipe the oil off his hands on his jeans. "Like that's going to work," Sarah said to herself, and picked up the old cloth she'd been using to clean the window earlier.

The car's owner obviously didn't hear her coming. When she tapped him on the shoulder, he visibly twitched as he turned round. "Here," Sarah handed him the cloth. "I saw you from my window over there. I thought maybe you needed a hand?"

He looked her up and down, hesitated, then took the cloth with a smile. The corners of his eyes wrinkled as he nodded his thanks. He was about her age, she realised, with a band of freckles that ran straight across the bridge of his nose. He looked ... familiar, somehow. Like a face in the crowd she'd passed once and couldn't quite place.

"Thank you," he said, wiping his hands on the towel. "I didn't realise I had an audience."

"I wasn't watching you," she said, too quickly. "I just heard the engine."

"It's loud, I know. I'm sorry. I'm working and it just ... fffft." He threw up his hands with an exasperated sound.

"How did you even get it up here? The roads are all blocked to cars, aren't they?"

"Most of them. I grew up here. There's a back way into the square. Shhh." He winked conspiratorially at her.

"You're from here?" Maybe that's why he looked so familiar – maybe they'd met one summer. She thought back through years of old memories, searching for a face that might fit.

"My whole life, I've been right here. It's not so good a story, is it? Not like yours." With a smile, he handed the towel back. "She's running again – for now. I have to go … but thank you."

"Maybe I'll see you round? I live there, on the corner. I've not been here that long: I don't really know many people…" Sarah tailed off. Why had she said that? And why had she said it to a complete stranger? What was she doing? She folded her arms across her chest, still holding the towel.

"Well," he said. "You know *me*, Sarah."

It was only as she watched the rear lights of the van bouncing off across the square that she realised she hadn't told him her name.

~~~

The knock on the door in the morning was a surprise. Bernez didn't usually knock: he usually just shouted a greeting as he let himself in, and if she wasn't there he made himself a cup of coffee and got on with whatever it was he was doing. Sarah didn't like unexpected knocks at the door. In her experience, they weren't usually the good kind.

A young woman stood on the doorstep, her eyes red and her skin pale. She was twisting a handkerchief round and around in her fist, and Sarah didn't even need to meet her eyes to know what had happened. Bernez's heart, it seemed, had finally given out on him in the night. His daughter knew they'd been "close" (and Sarah didn't like the emphasis she put on the word, but she let it pass) and had wanted to give her the news.

"Is there anything I can do?" Sarah asked, knowing what the answer would be. Her visitor simply shook her head and walked away, leaving Sarah to close the door and step back into a house that felt that little bit less complete.

There were other electricians, other plumbers, other builders … but none of them were Bernez. They were fine. They were bland and boring and beige, and they wouldn't dream of sitting in her favourite chair, smoking furiously, and telling her stories about the town. Bland. Boring. Beige. They were stories that she remembered in a part of her brain that itched from time to time: stories she knew she'd heard in the summers she had spent in Locronan. They were more than just stories: in some parts of Brittany, Bernez said, people still believed in them. The korrigans hiding in the hills and the devils who were waiting to trick unwary travellers out of their souls, or the kannerezed noz, who washed the clothes of the dead in the rivers and who, if seen, would demand that unfortunate passersby helped to wring out the cloth. But nowhere civilised believed in them anymore, Bernez would add, not in Cournouialle at least – before going on, always, to shrug and say that it might be different in

Penthièvre…

The house was emptier without Bernez's stories, without the smell of his cigarettes (which she found herself missing, against her better judgement) so she did her best to fill it with the sound of the loom. She was working on the cloth that had been left on the loom: going back to finish something that she'd started when she was barely big enough to move the beater. Jonny was excited about it, and the gallery had started talking about "concepts of memory" and "linear selves" and other things which had made Jonny even more excited. And Sarah? Sarah just … got on with it.

Emptier or not, the building was beginning to take on a more hospitable shape around her. There were reliable electrics now, the wires neatly pinned along the ceiling beams and channelled into the stone walls. The big granite fireplace in the main room and in the bedroom meant she didn't miss having central heating – not after a couple of months' practice of building a fire, anyway – and the worn flagstones of the ground floor were now covered in thick, warm rugs. She'd spent a whole weekend plaiting rope to hang through the metal loops set into the curved walls of the staircase. Something about the steps made her nervous, and having something to hold on to as she went up and down them made her feel a little more comfortable. Someone had obviously felt the same and had dropped something down them at one point, as there were a series of small, dark splashed stains on the stone, and a larger one at the bottom of the staircase. "What a waste of a bottle," Bernez had said, rubbing his beard, when she'd pointed it out and asked whether they'd be able to remove it. "But see it like this: it was a sacrifice for the house, no? Part of its history now. What good would it do to try and take it back?"

So she'd learned to live with the stains, just as she'd learned to love the slopes in the steps where generations of feet before hers had worn them down. Just as she was trying to learn to love the little stained glass window halfway up the stairs which someone had seen fit to draught-proof with molten candle wax. That was a harder thing to love, admittedly, but she was trying.

~~~

"You sound happier," Jonny said to her over the phone one night. She was huddled into the bench towards the top of the hill, looking down at the lights of the houses below, and trying to hang on to her mobile signal. "No. Maybe not happier. You're not allowed to be happy."

"Because happiness is a bad thing?"

"Nobody happy and well-adjusted ever made good art, darling. You know that."

"So what you're saying is that you need me to suffer."

"Absolutely. You're no good to me unless you're miserable."

"Jonny. Just leave it, would you?"

"What's wrong?" His tone immediately changed. All the banter was gone. "Sarah? What is it?"

"Nothing. I just … I don't know. Maybe it was a mistake coming back here. Maybe it's not right for me."

"Look. All I can tell you is what I know. And what I know is that you sound better. You're going to try and tell me you're as strung out as you were before you moved out there?"

"No…"

"And you're working again. How long had you been blocked?"

"I thought I didn't get blocked," she laughed.

He made a dismissive sound down the phone. "Your work, love. I'm serious. The photos you've sent over – they're beautiful. When do I get to see the actual piece?"

"When it's finished, Jon. Same as always."

They talked a little longer, with Jonny passing on gossip like he always did, and Sarah listening. Deep down, she already knew he was right. She was happier there. In a funny way, she felt like she belonged there more than she had anywhere else. She liked being able to look down on the town, to look at the lights spread out below her like a tapestry. And even as she thought it, she found herself planning a new piece. Grey for the houses and the cobbled streets, gold for the streetlights and deep, deep green for the moss that clung to the granite walls. Dark blue and black for the sky and the rainclouds, and white for the fog that curled through the streets. She could see the stripe of scarlet she would use for the car park, the slash of yellow for the cluster of light around the hypermarket on the far side of town. She could picture it as clearly as if it were on her loom in front of her. Of course Jonny was right.

She was already picking her way down the steep road back to the square, slippery in the cold night air, when she heard the familiar buzz of a 2CV engine again, coming from somewhere further up the hill behind her. Smiling to herself, she stepped to the side of the road and it wasn't long before the little van rattled past, then screeched to a halt. There was a grinding sound as the engine was forced into reverse and the van backed up alongside her. A familiar face smiled out of the window. "Hello again," he said.

"You know your headlights aren't working, don't you?" Sarah asked. Both the lamps on the front of the van were dark.

"I know where I'm going," he said with a shrug. "Cold night, no?"

"You didn't tell me you knew my name. You know mine, but I don't know yours."

"I told you. All my life has been spent here. I know everyone. Even when they only come for the summers."

"I knew it! We met when I was here with my father?"

"And you forget me. My heart!" He tapped a finger on his chest in a way that was so like Bernez, Sarah's own heart lurched. But the driver didn't seem to notice. "Maybe I was not so memorable. Yann. Yann Cariou." He held a hand out of the window to her, and she shook it, feeling oddly formal.

"Sarah Madec."

"You forget: I remember."

"It's nice to meet you, Yann Cariou." She shivered. The temperature was dropping, and already she could see wisps of fog beginning to build in the streets. "And now we're not total strangers, I don't suppose you'd give me a lift into town, would you?"

"Ah." His smile faded. "I'm sorry. Work, you know? Rules..." Through the window, she could see him shrug. "Besides, the van ... it's messy. Very messy."

She thought of the state of her car and smiled. "Mess doesn't bother me – but I wouldn't want to get you in trouble. Forget I asked."

"Are you in a hurry? Perhaps you have something you have to do?" There was a different question in his voice. She could hear it.

"No. I was just going back home. Up here's the only place I seem to be able to get a signal." She waved her phone at him. "My office," she said with a laugh, pointing back to the bench.

"It's not so bad," he smiled, looking past her into the gloom. "Perhaps I could make it up to you? I could buy you a drink?"

"Where, exactly, could you buy me a drink at this time of night?" She looked pointedly at her watch. Or where her watch would be if, in fact, she wore a watch. Which she didn't. And hadn't since she was fifteen. But he wouldn't know that, so.

"You break my heart and more than that, you turn me down?"

"I'm not turning you dow— Wait a minute. You're trying to make me feel bad, aren't you?"

He grinned at her from inside the van, but didn't answer.

"You're trying to make me feel bad, when you're the one leaving a lone woman stranded on the side of a mountain?"

He raised an eyebrow, and very deliberately looked up and down the street to make his point.

"Well, fine. It's still a mountain. Even if there's a town on it. And it's still cold. So there."

"A drink would warm you up."

"Which is all well and good, but the bar's closed and you know it."

"Another time, then. Goodnight, Sarah Madec."

"Goodnight, Yann Cariou," she said, shaking her head.

The engine revved again, and with a rattle he was gone.

~~~

She dug through the crates she hadn't yet emptied. There weren't many. There hadn't been that many to unpack in the first place. She travelled light, but there were still one or two things from the past she couldn't quite bring herself to part with and one of those was a wooden box full of photos. She spread them out across the rug in front of her bedroom fire and in the flickering light of the flames she sifted through them, a drink in her hand. There was the picture of her, six or seven years old, sitting on her father's knee at the loom; her fingers resting on the beater and her feet dangling high above the treadles. There was a picture of her in a blue cotton sundress, standing on tip-toe and peering into the wishing well; one of her watering the window boxes – older now, perhaps ten. A jump forward of another year or two saw her half in the shadows of the Fête de la Saint-Jean bonfire; another found her taking part in the grand *troménie*, her black dress clammy and itchy in the July sun. There she was, a little older in each one, looking out at herself sitting on the floor of this house again. Another photo – this time not of her. A woman in a long white dress and sandals, leaning against the side of the loom while her father worked. "Tante Barbe..." Sarah re-membered her. Her aunt – her father's older sister. It was *her* house, this house. They had come every year; every summer after her mother had left. Her father had packed them up and driven them here as soon as school finished, and they had stayed until the beginning of September. How they had all managed to fit into the narrow house, she didn't know. She'd never given it any thought at the time – all four of them crammed around the scrubbed wooden table in the kitchen, almost on top of each other and laughing as they passed bowls around.

Four.

She riffled through the pile of pictures, because suddenly she knew what she was looking for.

There was the picture of her at the loom, and there, peeping around the turn of the stairs, was a small face spattered with freckles.

There was the picture of her looking into the

wishing well, and there he was again: this time, sitting on the doorstep of the house, his hand shielding his eyes from the sun as he watched her.

There she was, watering the window boxes – and there was the familiar face looking down from the window above.

At the feu St Jean, he was beside her in the shadows, and at the *troménie* he was a few steps behind her.

Yann Cariou with his battered van.

Cousin Yann.

The same face followed her through the photos of her childhood, always watching over her. She remembered him now. She wasn't sure how she could have forgotten *him*, although she'd forgotten so much of it. He was older than she was by exactly a year. They even celebrated their birthdays on the same day. All the summers running in and out of the house with the town square as a playground; ducking through the wire fence and encouraging each other to balance along the girders of the half-built hypermarket. The time they dared each other to steal a bottle of local cider from the tourist shop and very nearly got caught, running and laughing and not daring to look back until they reached the graveyard; where they hid behind a crypt and drank the lot as the sun went down. That was when she'd fallen in love with the stories.

Just like Bernez, Yann told stories but his were darker even than Bernez's. His favourite, which he told her as they sat on a grave, passing her a flower from a funeral bouquet to put in her hair, was the Ankou: a skeletal figure who stalked the roads of old Brittany, collecting the souls of the dead. His cart was pulled by two horses, one fat and one thin, and he carried a scythe whose blade faced forward to reap the ghosts he was owed. "And his head? It turns. It always turns, round and round; so no death in the parish is hidden from him."

"Like *The Exorcist*?" she'd asked.

"Better." Yann laughed, dropping back to sit alongside her on the grave. She passed him the bottle and he took a long swig, wiping his mouth. "They say if you see him, you'll die within the year."

"Sounds like a stupid myth to me."

"Maybe. You don't live here."

"Do you know anyone who's seen him?

"Not that lived." He wiggled his eyebrows at her and grinned before clearing his throat and dropping his voice to a deep growl. "*Diouz a reoh, e kavoh.*"

"What's that supposed to mean?"

"According to your work, your reward."

"Again: what's that supposed to mean?"

"It means if you go looking for the Ankou, you might just find him."

Sarah felt a sudden chill, and then realised it was just Yann, blowing on the back of her neck. "I don't think that's what it's supposed to mean," she said, swatting him away.

"Who cares? Come on."

He drained the bottle and wedged it beside the nearest tombstone, jumping up and holding his hand out to her.

How could she have forgotten?

~~~

She almost didn't hear the knock at the door over the clatter of the loom. She had nearly finished the biggest of the pieces for the show, the final piece that had been missing: the single cloth left on the loom for twenty years. Time had faded the oldest threads and dust had found its way into the weave, giving it a greyish tint like something seen through fog. A black bar separated the old section from the new, which blazed with the brightest colours Sarah could lay her hands on. Jonny, when she'd sent the last photos through to him, made a loud squeak down the phone. This usually meant he was happy.

The knock came again, louder this time, and she sat back from the loom. The night had crept up on her, and although she'd lit the fire and switched on a handful of lamps around the room which kept it warm and cosy, she'd forgotten to close the shutters. Outside, she could see the streetlight swinging in the wind as raindrops splattered against the glass. Litter whirled across the cobbles of the square – which was never kept as neatly swept in November as it was in the summer when there were tourists to see it. And there was someone standing on her doorstep, wrapped in a long coat and wide-brimmed hat against the lashing rain.

Obviously catching the movement in the window, the hat tipped back – and there was Yann, smiling at her. She opened the door.

"You know who I am now, perhaps?" he asked, hopefully.

"Cousin Yann. I can't believe I didn't remember!" She smiled. "You'd better come out of the rain."

"I brought you a gift." He reached into the deep pockets of his coat and pulled out a bottle. "You still like cider, I hope?"

"It's the same one!" she laughed as he handed her the bottle. The liquid inside was heavy with sediment.

"I took two. I kept this one. In case." He shrugged off his coat and laid it on the stone window seat, where it dripped onto the floor. He dropped the hat on top of it.

"Nice hat," Sarah reached past him, about to pick it up, when somehow Yann managed to put himself between her and it, blocking her.

"Very wet. You don't want to. The rain." He nodded to the window, and for a second, his face was stern. But it was only a moment, and then his expression softened again. "You want me to close the shutters?"

"I'll get us some glasses." She set the bottle down on the table and edged around the loom towards the kitchen, picking a couple of glasses off the shelf. Seeing her, Yann scowled.

"Glasses? For cider? You've been too long away!" He dodged past the loom and elbowed her out of the way. "These!" he said, triumphantly holding up what looked like two small bowls. "Always these for cider."

"Oh, come on…"

"You think I'm old-fashioned? Fine. I am old-fashioned."

"I use those for soup."

"You always were a little ... odd."

"Odd? *Me?* I'm not the one driving that death-trap with no headlights." She folded herself onto the rug beside the fire. There wasn't really anywhere else to sit: only the seat at the loom and the chair that Bernez had liked to sit in, and she couldn't quite bring herself to sit in that somehow.

"I told you: I don't need them. I know where I'm going," said Yann with a shrug. He handed her a bowl of cider and stood in front of the chair. "You should sit."

"No, I'm fine here. I like being near the fire."

"I see." He narrowed his eyes at the chair, then shrugged and threw himself into it; almost spilling his drink in the process. "Ah, well. To family!" He lifted his bowl and drank, stretching his legs out in front of him. Sarah could smell the damp wool of his jumper drying in the warmth of the fire, and the scent of apples in the cider. The bottom two inches of his jeans were wet, as though he'd been striding through long grass, and there was old mud caked around the sides of his boots.

"You didn't tell me what you do in that van."

"Delivery driver."

"What are you delivering? Pizza?" She tried to stop herself from giggling. The drink was stronger than she'd been expecting: obviously all those years in a cellar hadn't done it any harm.

"Not pizza, no." He smiled at her. "You've almost

finished your drink. Here." He scooped the bottle up from the floor and she held out the little bowl for him to top it up. As he leaned back in the chair, his gaze swept the room and paused on the stains at the bottom of the steps. "You dropped something?"

"Not me. Whoever lived here between you and me, I suppose." It suddenly dawned on her. "Where do you live, anyway? Why isn't this *your* house now?"

"I couldn't stay here. A long story. Too long for this late at night, you know?" He shrugged and settled back into the cushions. "But I told you: my story, it's small and boring. You. Tell me about you – about this." He pointed at the loom. "Tell me."

So she did. She told him about the galleries, and her agent. She told him about her life since she'd spent her summers there with him; about art school and the awful jobs that came after it just to get by. How she'd met Jonny and how he'd got her her first spot in a show. How he told her she was on the verge of something, something big … and then, just like that, how the block came down between her and her work and she couldn't weave, couldn't paint, couldn't think. "It was like I couldn't see," she said, staring into the fire. "Like I've always been able to see, and then to see beyond that, to see something more, like the colours and the patterns in the world. And someone had taken that away."

Yann didn't respond. The only sound was the cracking of the wood in the fire and the wind outside.

"And then I got the letter about the house, and I came here … and it was like magic. Like it was meant to be." She looked round, half expecting him to be asleep, he was so quiet, but she was surprised to find him watching her intently. Studying her.

He set his bowl down gently on the floor. "Like it was meant to be," he said, and even though he smiled, he sounded sad. He tapped a finger on the arm of the chair. "I should go."

"Why?"

"I didn't think how late it was when I came. I should have thought: I don't want to keep you from this." He nodded towards the loom. "It matters to you so much."

"I didn't realise it. But yes. Yes, it does."

"So finish it." And before she could say another word, he had already swept his hat back onto his head and had thrown his coat back around his shoulders. "Finish it, because it matters."

As he let himself out, a gust of wind rushed through the open door and caught Sarah's hair, blowing it up and around her face and snuffing out the lighted candle on the windowsill.

~~~

The storm blew all night and through most of the next day, keeping her in the house. She worked, but even then, she knew her heart wasn't really in it. Threads snagged and tangled, and her feet slipped off the treadles and broke her rhythm. She washed the bowls they'd drunk from, turning his over and over in her hands in the water, and she must have knocked it somehow, because as she dried it on the cloth she realised it was cracked in a dozen places. It was lucky it hadn't leaked all over him. Maybe it had, and he was just too polite to say.

By the afternoon the storm had blown itself out and the world outside was quiet, still and fresh-washed by the rain. There wasn't a soul around. Everyone, just like her, was hiding from the weather. She pulled on her boots and her coat and wrapped her arms around herself and stepped down onto the wet street, climbing the hill to the back of town. But instead of turning right, along the little row of cottages that marked the very edge of the town, she turned left and followed the other road towards the graveyard. It wasn't somewhere she'd been intending to visit, admittedly, but she couldn't quite get the memory of that afternoon with Yann and the stolen cider out of her head, and she knew herself well enough to realise that until she went, that wasn't going to change. And until she *could* get it out of her head, she wouldn't be able to think about anything else.

The wrought iron gates had rusted over the years and they creaked as she swung one of them open. The paths were equal parts gravel and puddle, and she picked her way along between the graves. There were more than she remembered. Of course there were, given how much time had passed, and now the headstones rubbed shoulders with one another, some piled with gravel, some heaped with artificial flowers. She could almost hear the sound of her own running footsteps, crunching on the path years ago … could almost hear herself laughing as she raced after Yann. It didn't take her long to find the grave they'd sat on, the name almost worn away by time. There was no sign of the bottle: of course there wasn't. She hadn't expected to find it – it was probably cleared away within a day of them leaving it there. And yet. Seeing the one Yann had kept, it had given her an idea, to come to the graveyard to look for it. She'd imagined his face when she gave it to him.

Ah, well. Perhaps *that* wasn't meant to be.

With a smile, she doubled back towards the gate. The clouds were gathering again: maybe the storm hadn't quite finished with the town. As she pulled the gate closed behind her, a loose piece of gravel bounced up and caught in the hinge, jamming it. Sarah felt the first of the raindrops land on the back of her neck as she bent to pick it out, and shivered.

She saw it as she straightened up again, right at the edge of the row of plots.

A narrow stone, fresher than most of the others. The edges of the letters still sharp, the name so clear.

Roparz "Yann" Cariou.

Two dates were chiselled below it. The first, she knew all too well. It was almost exactly the same as her own birthday, with only a year's difference. The second was December 31st of the year before.

~~~

She wasn't surprised to see the little 2CV van parked outside the house, nor to see the figure in the long coat and broad hat standing on the doorstep.

"You know who I am now, perhaps?" he asked, just as he had the night before. But this time, his voice was solemn.

"I know who you are now," she said with a nod, and stepped past him to unlock the door. "You'd better come in."

He followed her inside, but this time, he did not take off his coat and he kept his hat on. It cast a shadow over his face, making him look haggard and pale.

"New Year's Eve," she said.

Beneath the brim of his hat, he nodded. "You remember the story, yes? The last to die in the parish, every year."

"Then what?"

"A year. A year as *oberour ar maro*. I collect, I deliver. One year. And then ... who knows?"

"What happened?"

"I fell. Nothing more. I slipped, I fell." He pointed to the stain at the bottom of the stairs. "It was New Year's Eve, after all, and I was alone. No-one knew until it was already too late."

"This *is* your house. I asked why you didn't live here."

"I *did* live here. I left it to you. You received the letter from my lawyer, no?"

"I didn't recognise the name ... you were always Yann."

"If you were called Roparz, wouldn't you change it?" There was the faintest glimmer of a smile in the shadows beneath the hat.

"So ... you died."

"Everyone does. It's not such a rare thing, Sarah."

"And me? What about me?"

"What about you?"

"But you always said … the Ankou…"

"The Ankou comes for the souls of the dead. The first night we talked, I was here for your friend, Bernez. It was his time," he added softly, seeing the look on her face. "When it's time, it's time. My time, your time. It's never ours to begin with. It's borrowed. And all things borrowed must be returned."

"I'm not dead."

"You're not, it's true." He shrugged.

"So why are you here?" She found herself edging behind the loom, wanting to put something between them. Yann wasn't Yann any more. He seemed taller, thinner; he took up both more and less space than he should, and the room felt cold.

"Family. You, Sarah, are family." He held a hand out towards her, and like his face, it was paler and thinner; the fingers longer than any hand she'd ever seen, with knuckles that looked like stones. "What else does the Ankou do? Remember, Sarah. I need you to remember."

She held onto the frame of the loom. There was a splinter pressing into her palm but she didn't dare let go, didn't dare move. She remembered the graveyard, the sunset, the summer. She remembered the taste of apples, the cool of Yann's shadow as he spread his arms wide while he talked.

"They say if you see him, you die within the year."

"Family, Sarah. Because you are family, I came to warn you." He drew himself up, taller again than anyone could possibly be, and he pulled his hat down from his head. Long, white hair tumbled down his back from beneath it, and behind her she heard every piece of crockery in the kitchen shatter. The shards tinkled as they fell from the shelves to the floor, breaking into little more than dust on the hard stone. The Ankou's coat swirled around him and the deep pockets which had held a bottle were full of bones. They clattered as he stepped towards her. She moved further around the loom. "You have a year."

"And then?"

"And then … the Ankou comes."

"Will it be you?"

"No." He shook his head. "My year is almost up. The next Ankou may not be so kind. He will not warn you."

"What about you?"

"A year I serve. A year I collect and deliver. After that, who knows?" He was repeating himself. He didn't know what came next. He didn't seem to care, either, standing calmly in the house that had been his – the house where he had died – holding his hat in his hands.

"A year. It was always all that separated us, yes?" He waited for her to answer. She didn't: she had nothing to say. So he shrugged and he lifted his hat back onto his head, and the long white hair curled itself tightly beneath the brim. "Finish your work, Sarah. It matters."

"Why does it matter if I've only got a year left?"

"Because it matters to you."

"And I'm going to die."

"Everyone dies, Sarah. Everyone. Only this..." he waved at the fabric on her loom; the weaving begun years before and almost finished, spanning her whole life. "Only this has a chance. *This* remains."

"It's just cloth."

"Just cloth." He waved a hand over it and as she watched, the warp and the weft unwound themselves and floated apart, then spun back together faster and faster. "Just cloth," he said again, running his finger down the length of the fabric. With a flick of his wrist, he had rewoven her work into a shroud. "More than 'just cloth'," he said pointedly, and flicked his wrist again. The fabric was the same as it had always been.

The door swung open, letting the darkness of the gathering storm inside. He stopped in the doorway, his back to her. She stepped out from behind the wooden frame, unable to stay there any longer.

"Finish it, Sarah. Finish it and be ready. He'll come. And after that, maybe I'll see you again. Who knows?" He turned to look back at her one more time – and this time, the face under the hat was unmistakably Yann's, as young and friendly as it had been that summer. "Diouz a reoh, e kavoh," he said, and the door closed behind him.

Outside, she heard the engine of the 2CV start up, but right before it did she could have sworn she had heard the sound of horses' hooves shuffling on the cobbles of the square.

And as the sound of the old van faded into the night, Sarah took a deep breath and turned to face her loom.

INAPPETENCE

Steve Rasnic Tem

They slipped from the shadows to monitor his decline. Impatient, they moved forward to taste the light. All the world was hungry it seemed, except for him. Even the thought of food repelled him.

Guy stared at the spoon his daughter Ann had shoved up to his face. The yellow glop sitting there glistened with a pre-digested sheen. "I can't." He turned his head away.

"He's just like Princess was," a small voice said. One of his grandchildren, he wasn't sure which. One of the girls maybe. "She didn't eat anything for over a week. And then she— The vet took her away and we never saw her again."

"Inappetence. That's what the vet called it. She couldn't eat. They look at the food but they can't eat the food. They're just not interested. It was because of her teeth. Are Grandad's teeth okay? I know he doesn't have them all, but he has some. But how are the rest of them? Maybe his mouth hurts and that's why he won't eat."

That was Tony, who'd just started college. Tony was a bright kid, and Guy loved him, but the boy always had an explanation for everything. Young people needed to learn how to listen. You can't listen if you're always talking. Guy didn't talk much anymore. But he was listening all the time. He turned his head and looked forward again, but kept his mouth clamped shut in case his daughter tried something sneaky with the spoon.

His vision was blurry. They were all standing there, he thought, at the foot of his bed and around the side, so many of them. He and Cassie had raised a huge brood. Their bodies were far brighter than anything else in the room, except their faces which were shadowed or blurred – he wasn't sure – at least out of sync with the rest of them. He couldn't make out individual facial features, so he was unable to tell them apart.

"Let Ann help you, Dad." That was Robert's voice, his oldest. Jimmy was somewhere in that bunch as well, and Jimmy's wife. They all let Ann take the lead. Ann was like her mother, always taking charge when someone was sick.

He loved his children and grandchildren, all of them. But he had no appetite for them right now, or anyone else. He had to figure out what was going on with him, with his world, and it seemed he didn't have much time. He might not understand a lot of things, but he recognised when time was running out.

He felt an itch somewhere on his right leg, but he couldn't pin it down. Even if he knew its exact location, he had no way to scratch it. He imagined his skin was breaking down, little bits of it falling off everywhere. It was the sort of thing you normally didn't think about. But at this stage of his life most of the things he thought about were entirely new to him.

Ann held his hand. "Dad, if you can't eat, your doctor will put you back in the hospital. I know you don't want that. None of us do."

He shook his head. "Water. Please."

A straw poked at his mouth. He grabbed it with his lips and sucked the cool liquid in. So delicious. When he was done, he pushed the straw away with his tongue. His eyes cleared momentarily, and he saw it was one of the boys, Jude, who was holding the glass. "Good boy." He smiled and Jude smiled back. Such a handsome boy. Guy didn't think he had ever been that handsome even for one day. Why Cassie agreed to marry him he had no idea.

He began to choke. He couldn't catch his breath. Things went flying out of his mouth and he felt intensely dizzy. He heard a couple of the children crying and a rush of activity. Someone propped him up and held a cloth under his chin. Something came out of his mouth, mostly phlegm, but maybe something else. He wondered if he'd lost a piece of tongue, some bit of throat lining, a tonsil perhaps, or something deeper. Did he still have his tonsils? Probably not. At the moment he couldn't remember exactly what tonsils were.

The sudden trauma cleared both his head and his vision, and apparently the room, as only his daughter and Tony remained. "What? Did somebody die?"

"Dad!" Ann leaned forward in the chair by the bed, her cheeks damp and her eyes shadowed with exhaustion. Beside her was the table stacked with his vast repertoire of pills and other medicines.

Tony's face looked stricken. Guy felt terrible. "Oh, I'm sorry kiddo. That was just a stupid joke. I meant no harm."

"S-okay," Tony said. He was trying to smile but failing. Guy imagined the boy didn't want to be there, but he was sticking to his guns, acting like an adult. Good for him.

Guy shifted his head and gazed at his daughter. "Could I rest a while, honey? Try again at dinner? Some Jell-O maybe?"

"Dad, that *was* Jell-O."

"Maybe a different colour then, if we have it."

"Sure. We've got all the colours of the rainbow down there." She kissed him on the cheek and they left the room.

He wasn't sleepy. He wanted to be by himself for a while. He couldn't look at their eager faces wanting him to be better. He couldn't tell them he was done.

He had a big house and didn't mind they'd moved in downstairs. In fact, he wished they'd done it sooner when he'd been healthy enough to enjoy their company. Most days he could barely hear them. The murmur of their conversations might as well have come from next door or even down the street.

Sometimes there were gentle vibrations emanating from below. He liked to imagine they were from children joyfully playing. Sometimes cooking smells drifted up the three flights of stairs and into his room. These were not welcome as they triggered nausea almost instantly. Guy couldn't even think of food. Everything meant for consumption seemed poisonous now.

This room at the top of the house had windows all around. It was octangular and clung to the corner of the structure, hanging slightly above the third floor. When he and Cassie bought this place, they called this room the lighthouse. Sometimes when they took walks at night they'd come back and see its windows from a block away, all lit up and showing them the way home. "It looks so full of life," Cassie would say. "I bet some very happy people live in that house."

She'd used this room as her art studio. That was her painting hanging high on the wall above the foot of the bed: a natural bower of trees by a stream rendered in layers of olive green and umber and russet shadow. Every day Guy stared at the painting and thought he saw something different arriving in the gloom beneath the trees. This disturbed him, and yet he often thought about lying down in such a place and waiting for whatever was to come. Something stealing out of the shadows. Something rising out of the water along the bank. It unsettled him to think this way, but he couldn't help himself.

Several of the windows were open to facilitate a nice cross breeze. Cassie had liked it this way and Guy wanted to recreate at least some of the ambiance. He had plenty of blankets on the bed, but his daughter complained he would get too cold. He let her close most of the windows at night rather than argue.

He heard a car door slam. Probably Ann's husband

Mark coming home from work. He was a good man and treated them all well. He told Guy tales of the progress he'd made with various household repairs and remodelling, because he recognised this was news Guy would appreciate hearing. But death embarrassed Mark, and of that they did not speak.

He could hear the kids playing outside, the crisp sounds they made as they stepped on the first fallen leaves, the random exchanges between neighbours he hadn't talked to in months. He might have been able to get himself up with the walker and use it to get over to the window and look out, maybe even call down a word or two, but he might fall, and ruin the evening for everyone. Besides, he didn't want to see how the colours had changed, how activities were still taking place without him, how life still maintained its same, inevitable pace. The world outside was still hungry. People were still starving to do things, to eat their time away. But Guy had no more appetite.

Late afternoon shadow slipped into the room and spread across the floor. Despite its placement high on the house, this room went dark first due to the placement of the nearby trees. But it was the beginning of autumn, and once the leaves were off the trees and spread across the ground, he'd see bare limbs and the steel clarity of winter light again, assuming he lived that long.

He wouldn't mind getting to hear the crunch of all those leaves again, the kids kicking them swish swish swish as they came home from school. He'd always enjoyed that particular sound, and the explosive crush when one them dived into a thick pile.

Ann came up with a plate as it turned dark. He saw the shiny green of the lime Jell-O, and at least his stomach didn't react. She sat next to him and asked if he wanted to feed himself. He sat up, but his hand was too weak to securely hold the spoon. He hadn't expected that and didn't know how to feel about it. She fed him a few spoonfuls, and he relished the slight tang of flavour, but then his stomach clenched. She pushed the emesis basin under his chin just in time.

After she'd cleaned him up and he could speak, he said, "We'll try it again in the morning." He tried to smile but didn't know if he had actually succeeded at creating one.

She kissed him on the forehead. "Light on or off?"

"On for now. But could you check on me later? I mean, if I should fall asleep, you could switch the light off. I hate wasting electricity. The planet, you know?" He didn't want her to know he was scared, but perhaps she already did.

"Of course, Dad." The sounds of her descending steps went on for a long time.

He thought about the creamy white stuff they fed you in the hospital, when you couldn't or wouldn't eat. They filled a thick plastic bag with the stuff and hung it from a pole. They inserted a line directly into your chest, and the white stuff ran down the tube and fed you through there. He didn't want that. He tried to imagine eating without tasting or smelling, without using his mouth or nose at all.

He wanted to talk to Ann about Hospice, but he

didn't know how to bring up the subject. Ever since she was a little girl, he'd always hated disappointing her. The look on her face broke him every time.

The wind picked up. Cassie's painting rattled against the wall. He thought he saw movement inside the bower, something coming out to the stream to drink, or going back into the shadows to hide. But the painting was shaking, the wind trying to lift it off the wall, so possibly that was all.

He could hear the trees outside creaking and bending, the branches shaking, the sharp crackle of dead leaves as more began to fall. The yard must have been swimming with them. Both the open and the closed windows were clattering within their frames.

He began to smell the corruption. He was sure it wasn't him. He'd worried a great deal about his personal hygiene during his illness, whether they could help him stay clean enough so he wouldn't stink. He didn't want his grandkids to remember him as a smelly old man. He didn't know exactly what the odour was but it wasn't any smell he knew a human body made. The stench was somewhere outside the window.

He heard them moving through the leaves. He thought he might have been hearing them for several minutes but he'd been focused on the wind and Cassie's painting. He had no idea how many of them there were. The crunching leaves made it sound like an army.

Guy couldn't understand why they were so impatient. Perhaps he wasn't meant to understand.

But they could have waited until he stopped breathing. Maybe people who were dying gave off a particular scent or emanation that drew them. Maybe they couldn't help themselves. That was what he wondered when he first saw one, the one bony shoulder and the side of its pale unformed face in the open window a few weeks ago.

He'd had a suspicion, so he asked Tony to read to him from a couple of books in his lawyer's bookcases. They would be Tony's eventually, along with everything else in the cramped office space which had been his retreat for decades. He'd made that clear to Ann even though she struggled as much as possible not to talk to him about the *after.* "He can use some of the supplies at the university, and maybe later he'll want to dig into my library, maybe even build one of his own," he'd told her. "I know he likes to read. He's a smart kid. I'm proud of him, tell him that. Tell him he can have anything in my office he wants. It's all his."

Tony was not the most patient lad, but he seemed to enjoy reading to Guy. He'd read well, with no stumbles. "From Arabic mythology. Ghoul or Ghul. Ghouls feed on human flesh, drink blood, rob graves, prey on corpses, etc. It also refers to a person who revels in the loathsome and revolting. I think I know some people like that."

"I think we all do. What does the other book say?"

"There are some pictures, but they're all over the place in terms of conception and approach. Your basic hideous creature, I guess, whatever that means to you."

"That's okay. I can use my imagination. Anything else?"

"Um. Drinks blood, we already knew that. Steals coins. Wait. 'Shape-shifts into an ostrich'."

"You're making that up!"

"No Grandad – it's right here." He started to hand over the book.

"I'll take your word for it. I'm not seeing that well these days. Go on."

Tony skimmed the page with his finger. "Sometimes preys on lonely travellers or children."

"What does it say about that?"

"That's all. It's the last line of the article. Maybe if it can't find a corpse it eats whatever's handy. If you like I can see if I can find out more on the internet. Why are you interested in this Dungeons and Dragons stuff anyway?"

"I remember hearing the word, and Halloween's coming up. Have you picked out a costume yet? You could go as a ghoul or whatever."

"Grandad, the last time I dressed up for Halloween I was twelve, and even then I was embarrassed."

Guy remembered smiling at that bright and lovely boy. There was probably nothing to worry about. When the body was stuck in bed the mind had nothing better to do than to imagine the worst things possible. In any case, that was folklore. Even if he had seen something to worry about, the reality was likely far different than the human interpretation.

He heard scrambling on the brick outside. He began sweating profusely. He was being ridiculous. He knew prolonged bed rest sometimes resulted in psychological stresses besides the usual physical complications. Decreased concentration, orientation, and intellectual skills. Anxiety, depression, irritability – he'd experienced all those. Occasional hallucinations.

Then there was the smell again, originating from some rotten mouth, a corrupted gut. He hated to think Cassie might have experienced any of this during her final days. With all his being he hoped not. She'd been unconscious most of her last two weeks. Of course, he didn't know what she'd dreamed about during that time. He liked to think it was of a peaceful afternoon under the trees beside a stream, with nothing hiding in the shadows except more green.

The light went out. Had Ann come up and flipped the switch? Had he dozed off? He listened for footsteps on the stairs but heard none. From the spirited sounds of the wind, possibly they'd lost power. He wondered if she would try to check on him.

A shush of sound, and maybe something sliding over the windowsill. He felt an anxious itching in his extremities with no apparent location, a vague sort of nibbling.

A scramble and a crawl and he thought he would scream. He stared at the foot of the bed. The painting hanging above was swallowed in shadow. He had no taste for this. He wasn't cut out for it.

They stood up with all their blank faces, hairless bodies emaciated and vaguely doglike, their long fingers ending in sizable claws. He listened again for footsteps on the stairs and hoped not to hear them. He needed his family most of all to stay away.

For a moment his brain skipped, and he was back in the hospital bed with no appetite left for anything, the doctors towering above him, discussing his case as if he weren't there. He'd wanted to shout and tell them he could hear every word.

Then back in his own bed, in the lighthouse at the top of his world, the blank faces looming closer, then as if to tease him, the faces becoming his own, except with the hunger returned.

"Just do it!" he shouted. "Do your damn job!"

And they did.

MEETING AT THE SILVER DOLLAR

Marion Pitman

It was early, too early for the whores and gamblers to be awake, but one man sat in the Silver Dollar saloon: watching the door, holding a silver dollar, throwing it up and catching it. He wore an overcoat, it being a cold day, but as his arm moved you could see a silver star pinned to his vest. There was a bottle of whiskey on the table in front of him, but he was drinking coffee.

Tucson Charlie, the bartender, was sweeping the floor, and gradually lifting all the chairs down and settling them around the tables. He glanced round frequently at the door, and at the man with the star.

Charlie had got to the back of the room when a figure appeared at the swing doors. The man with the star looked up, his hand dropping the dollar on the table and moving to his side; but he halted the movement when he saw the one who walked in.

Not even a man, he thought: a boy; hardly growing a beard yet. Seventeen or so? But sharply dressed, and the Colt that hung from his hip was business-like.

The boy pushed open the swing doors, stepped

through and stood pat. The man with the star looked him up and down.

The boy said, "Are you looking at me, mister?"

"Ain't no-one else here, boy. No offence. I'm waiting for someone, but you ain't the one I'm waiting for. Sit down; take a drink."

Charlie, looking nervous, brought over a couple of glasses. The boy hesitated, then sat, keeping the chair back a little from the table, hand hovering over his gun.

The man with the star poured two glasses of whiskey, pushed one across the chipped polish of the table. The boy took it, sipped the rough liquor. He seemed to be used to drinking. He took another sip, and said, "Who are you waiting for?"

"Feller called Dan Morris. And I have to tell you, son, if he turns up, things are likely to get lively around here."

"Well, I guess I ain't afraid of that. And don't call me son. I'm nineteen; I'm a man."

"Well, son, you'll have to forgive me, but I'm forty six, and you sure look more like a boy to me. Now don't get riled up. I can see you know how to handle yourself. Where you from? If'n you don't mind my asking."

"I'm from West Texas. Concho County."

"Uh-huh. You're a long way from home."

"Had to leave. I killed a man in a fight. But it suits me; I'm aiming to see the world, make me some money; see something of life."

"Yeah? You go round talking about killing people,

and wearing that pistol the way you do, you're more likely to see something of death."

"Not me. Why, I'm the fastest gun in Concho County."

"Is that right? Is that how you killed that feller, with a gun?"

"Yes sir. He insulted my sister, and I called him out. He hadn't hardly cleared leather when I shot him."

"How many men you killed, altogether?"

"Uh – just the one, so far. Why?"

"Well, you got time to stop. Couple more, that's it: you have to go on."

"Why should I want to stop? I mean, I ain't a murderer, but there's people out there – bad people – that need stopping, even if I have to kill them."

The man with the badge shook his head. He'd heard it so many times before, from so many men and boys that were out there now in Boot Hill, or on their way there. He sighed. "So, son – mister – what you doing here, in my town?" He moved his arm as he said it, and the boy caught sight of the badge on his vest.

The boy sat up a little straighter; "Are you the sheriff?"

"Guess I am."

"Well – I'm sorry – I guess I've been talking out of turn a little. But that guy I shot, it was a fair fight. I mean, I'm not wanted. I'm not on the run. Only thing was, his folks was after me, and I had to clear out for a while; so I figured it was a good chance to get out and see something of the world. You know what I mean?

Okay. So, what am I doing in your town? I'm looking for a man named Frank Davis."

The sheriff was very still for a moment, then he said, "Yeah? So who's Frank Davis, and why do you want to find him?"

"You mean you never heard of Frank Davis? I thought everyone'd know Frank Davis. Why, he's my hero. He faced down the Cosker gang and beat them single-handed; he cleaned up Grover with just one old man and a boy; he's brought the law to half the towns in the West. I can't believe you never heard of him!"

The boy heard the barman behind him give a kind of snort, and he narrowed his eyes at the man with the star; "You have heard of him. You're just making fun of me."

"I wouldn't do that, son. But you're wrong, Frank Davis ain't no hero. And I ought to know."

"Why? How would you know? Who are *you*?"

The barman laughed, and the man with the star said, "I'm Frank Davis."

The boy gaped. "You – you're – *you're* Frank Davis?"

"Uh-huh. And I ain't no hero. You want to know the truth? I faced the Coskers single-handed – sure. With six men backing me up from the roof of the hotel and the church and the window over the dry goods store. I cleaned up Grover – but it was pretty clean already, most of the riff-raff had moved on when the silver ran out.

"As for the law – that's my job, boy. I'm paid for it and I do it. Dan Morris is coming to get me, because I arrested him for bank robbery, and he's just done four years in the State prison. If he draws on me, I'll kill him or he'll kill me, but the world won't be a better place, either way.

"I'm not a hero, boy. If I ever had any interest in being a hero, I left it with my brother under the peach trees at Shiloh. You understand me?"

"You were a soldier?"

"Sure I was. And let me tell you, a soldier ain't a hero. A soldier's just a damn fool."

"I can't believe that."

"A soldier's a man that goes out to kill or get killed for someone else's idea. A lawman goes out to get killed for wages. Neither of them is a hero. A hero's a man that raises crops or cattle, and marries a decent woman and raises kids, and feeds them and teaches them right from wrong. If there were more heroes like that, there wouldn't be no need for soldiers and lawmen. Hear what I'm telling you, son?"

"I hear you, Mr Davis. But – I guess I don't quite see it that way. Seems to me there's always going to be bad men, and someone has to stand up against them."

"That's a fact. But it ain't nothing to be proud of. And it ain't something to hanker after. Once you're up there, standing against them, you're a target for the rest of your life. You understand that? You're a hero today, maybe; but when the town quietens down and gets respectable, and they pull down the whorehouse and build a church— Charlie, what you sniggering at?"

"Pull down the whorehouse? No town ever gets

that respectable."

"Well, they move it out of town. Will you shut up? I'm trying to save this kid's life. OK, so they get respectable, and then they realise they've got this gunslinger cluttering up the sheriff's office, making the place look untidy, and they start hinting that there's other towns need cleaning up; sheriff, no offence, and eventually they run you out of town. That's why I keep moving on. Not because I have some divine mission to bring law to the West – I just keep getting run out of town.

"That ain't no way to live, boy."

"I – I dunno, Mr Davis. I don't guess I'm cut out for farming, and it ain't much life being a ranch hand. I hear what you're saying, but – hell, I'm good with a gun. There's got to be some way to use that."

"Well, I sure don't know any way to use being good with a handgun that doesn't involve shooting people. And I've shot a lot of people, and I don't say any of 'em was much loss, but then again, what have I got to show for it? If Dan Morris kills me today, there won't be nothing left behind, except a few dime novel stories that don't tell the truth."

"But he ain't going to kill you, Mr Davis. You're the best there is."

"Look, boy, if you tell anyone this, I'll deny it; but I'm slowing down. That's the other thing that happens – you slow down. You can't help it. Unless you die young, you get old. My reactions are slowing, my hand just plumb don't move like it used to. Maybe I'll kill Dan; and maybe he'll kill me. If I get lucky today, maybe I won't the next time. You follow me? Sooner or later, someone's going to be quicker. You just wait for that time. And mostly you wait on your own.

"I tell you, boy, get a job on a cattle drive, or go out prospecting, or, hell, even get a job tending bar. But don't try getting into the hero business. It don't pay near as well as you think."

"Hell, Mr Davis, I don't know what to say. I still think you're a damn fine man, but – hell—"

"And don't cuss so much. You're too young."

"What? Uh—"

Charlie said, "He don't like to hear people cuss. It's the way his Ma brought him up."

"Shut up, Charlie."

The boy stammered a bit, then said, "Look, Mr Davis, seems to me if what you're saying is true, anyone might be faster than you. Anyone. Even me."

The sheriff's eyes narrowed; "You want to try it, boy? Cos I tell you, the fastest gun in Concho County ain't necessarily the fastest gun anywhere else. And I ain't slowed down *that* much."

"Uh – he— Heck no, Mr Davis. I didn't mean that!"

"You was thinking it though. You was thinking, hell, if that's true, if I can out-gun my hero, don't that make me a hero? Wasn't you, son?" He sounded more sad than angry.

The boy reddened; "I wouldn't do that, Mr Davis. I – I respect you. And I see what you're doing. You reckon to talk me out of what I'm set on, because, well, I guess you ain't sure I've got what it takes. But I have. I have got what it takes. I know it'll mean always having to be the best, having to watch my back, never resting; but I'm willing to do that, if I can make the world safer and more decent."

"You ain't listening," said the sheriff. "It don't make the world any safer or more decent. What makes a town, and the world, decent, is if enough of the folks in it want it to be decent. Ain't a thing a man with a gun can do about that. And without that, don't matter how many bad *hombres* you send to meet their maker, there'll always be just as many to take their place. Do you understand now?"

Charlie said, "Give it up, son. He's got twenty-five years start on you in the arguing business. And he's right. If people ain't behind the law, it can't work; and if they are, it shouldn't need six-guns to back it up. Of course, it doesn't always actually work out that way, but that's sure the way to bet. You might make a difference, or you might not, but you'll never know, and you'll never be thanked even if you did."

"Charlie, will you let me do this my way? Being disillusioned by your hero is one thing; being disillusioned by a bartender is just damned embarrassing."

The boy tried to suppress a grin, and the sheriff said, "He's right about the last bit. You'll never know if you made things better or worse, or made no difference; and you sure as hell won't get any gratitude."

"I ain't looking for gratitude," the boy protested, taking another drink of whiskey to mask his confusion. "But when you say you never know if you made things better or worse – is that true?"

"True for me, true for most people I know. Listen, son, if you really want to be rootless all your life, never have a wife and kids to come home to, never have a place to *call* home, never to have a friend you know you can trust, always tell your troubles to bartenders because they're the only people who'll listen, because listening is their job— What is it, Charlie?"

"I hear the noon train coming in, sheriff. The train Dan Morris'll most likely be on."

"Thanks, Charlie. Listen, son, you better clear out. You don't want to be caught in the cross-fire—"

"Look out!"

The boy's voice, the crash of glass, the sound of two shots, and a second, smaller crash, came so hard upon each other they seemed like just one sound. Then the boy was on his feet; Charlie was coming up from under the bar with a shotgun, glancing at his shattered mirror; Frank Davis was half turned in his chair, and a man was lying bleeding in the gap of a broken window at the side of the room.

The sheriff stood up and walked across the bar; Charlie said, "Might be more of them outside," and kept the shotgun trained on the window, with an eye also to the swing doors.

The sheriff looked out of the window, then bent to the man lying across the sill, his hand, still holding the gun, hanging down on the floor, his head against the wall, his legs grotesquely still in the street. "It's Dan Morris; and he's dead." He looked out once more;

"Looks like he was alone. Boy—" he turned around; "—I take it back. You *are* good."

The boy stood still, his face dead white, the six-gun still in his hand. "Uh. Thank you. He— I just saw him as he—"

"You saved my life." The sheriff's voice was flat, a little bleak. "I honestly don't know if I'm glad or sorry."

"Yeah. I mean – I didn't think. It just happened."

Charlie the bartender said, "There'll be people here soon. What are we going to tell them?"

The sheriff and the boy looked at each other.

Charlie went on, "If Frank Davis shot Dan Morris, that ain't news. That's what everyone expects. If a Texan boy no-one's heard of shot Dan Morris and saved Frank Davis's life, that's news. Either of you want to be news?"

There was a silence that lasted half a minute and felt like half a lifetime. The sheriff said, "I guess it has to be up to you, boy. Maybe I'm wrong, after all, and this is what you should be doing."

The boy shook his head violently. "No. No, I – hell, I feel sick. I mean, I'm glad I saved your life, Mr Davis, even if you're not; but I don't, I don't want to make my living shooting strangers. That's just... You're right, that ain't no way to live." He holstered his gun, sat down, and took another slug of whiskey.

The sheriff said, "Charlie, did you see what happened?"

"Not me, sheriff, I didn't see a thing. My eyesight's so bad I never do, you know that. I'm deaf, too."

There were people, now, at the doors, looking over, sussing out the situation; the first to come in was the undertaker, Nathan Black.

"Sheriff. You got me another customer?"

"That's right, Nath. Dan Morris got what he was looking for."

"Reckon he slipped off the train early and stole a horse. Figured he'd fool you, take you by surprise. Ed saw him sneaking up the side of the saloon, but there wasn't nothing we could do."

"I guess there never is. Take him away, Nath, bury him proper. The town'll have to foot the bill."

"Ain't no sneaking up on you, sheriff. You're a real hero."

"Sure. Sure I am, Nathan. Take him away. And get someone to come fix that window, there's a hell of a draught."

DRAGON-FORM WITCH

Joyce Chng

She backs away from the dagger, as if it is a live snake, like one of the painted bronzebacks basking in the garden. The dagger is shaped like a Lung, its body a wavy and sharp blade. Its hilt is all taloned claws.

And its pommel is its head. Green jade gives its eye an unnatural ethereal cast.

"Take this," ah-ma says. "It's yours now."

"No…"

She stares at the blade as it rests lightly and flat on her open palm. It feels warm. The blade belonged to her grandfather. The blade *is* her grandfather. His blood and soul were part of what forged it.

She is Lung, like ah-ma. But holding a dragon-form dagger unnerves her. Using it as her ritual athame terrifies her.

"Take this. Fight the darkness for us."

She sees ah-ma's dragon form – a silver ti lung – curling up before her. This earth lung is old, weary. Fierce eyes pin her down, like an eagle eyeing its prey. She blinks and she sees ah-ma's frail elderly body once more, clothed in dark blue *samfoo* and pants.

"I can't…" She whispers, knowing that her excuse will be ignored. She has spent the whole of her childhood coming up with excuses.

The darkness comes at her, fast, a black oily blur.

She has no time to perform the lengthy ritual to call the four dragons. All she does is to hiss a quick prayer and visualize a flaming circle around herself. Her Wiccan mentors will laugh at her. She is mixing and merging different traditions together.

The four dragons are wholly hers. The orange-hued dragon for the East, the watery-blue dragon for the West. The North dragon, all ice and winter, came to her in a dream, a tian lung wreathed in icicles and frost. It's the controller of winter storms, its tail the relentless sweep of winter winds. The South dragon is all fire, like the flames from ah-ma's paper money offerings, swirling bright and hot.

But, not now. She has no time.

The darkness has a gaping maw for a mouth. She has heard her ah-ma and aunts call this type of darkness a "hunger". They prey on emotions, almost like the *jiang shi* who *eats* blood.

She draws her athame, sweeps it in an arc, keeping it in front of her. She made Kim teach her the basics of dagger play and even then, she has probably messed up all of them.

The dagger cuts a vivid red curve in the air and power rushes up her right arm, like fire, like ice. With a roar like an earthquake, the red form of a ti lung emerges from the dagger, claws out and fanged jaws bared. Its beard flows like the back-draft of fire. She is filled with immense power.

"Come at me," she challenges the darkness and her

voice resonates. Her grandfather bolsters her strength.

The darkness screams. It wants to eat her, but is wary of the fire and magic. It knows who she is and what she is capable of.

She doesn't wait for it to react. She launches herself at it, all black, night given form, her dagger slashing downwards. Its tip pierces it and burns its way through. The darkness's howl fills her ears. She doesn't care. She feels as if she is on fire, a huo lung in flight.

When she hits the ground, the darkness dissipates. The howl of pain lingers in the air. There is the smell of burning and ash.

She breathes hard, trying to stop the vertigo and the sudden weakness in her limbs. Her head throbs, slowly transforming into a migraine.

Her phone beeps. "Iron Man" by Black Sabbath. Her favourite ringtone. It is loud in the silence.

"Yin Tian. Come home. Very urgent."

Her mother.

She settles down gracefully at the water's edge, calmed by the mirror-flat surface. The night whispers about her. Lights, like fireflies so rare in Singapore now, sparkle about her. Somewhere she hears the throb of techno and smells the whiff of barbequed chicken wings. A girl's soft giggle comes from the grove of Portia trees, followed by soft masculine murmurs. She loves the night and it loves her back.

"You are early tonight." The ice-cold hand touches her shoulder and she looks up to see the water spirit looming above her. She can see the stars and a random passing plane through the transparent figure.

"I was relieved early from my duties," she explains, always feeling edgy around the water spirit. The spirit flows, like the slow cascade of clear water. It moves in the shape of a woman, the shape it wants to be seen by mortal eyes.

"No more deaths," the water spirit whispers softly and ripples as if it shudders in revulsion. "I am glad. Stopping the hungers tires me."

"Thank you for your help."

The water spirit sighs. "The hungers were drawn to the sadness. So much sadness, so much pain. Your people are in pain. Can they find solace?"

She remembers all the news in the papers. The suicides. The drownings. A society in flux and eating itself from inside out.

"No."

"Why? There is so much beauty here. Why is there pain, little mortal?"

The throb of techno grows suddenly loud and there is drunken laughter, a sharp-pitched yelping. She feels the change of atmosphere, the feeling of hunger in the air, the emptiness in her stomach. She stiffens, almost reaching for her dragon-form athame in her pocket. She finds it difficult talking about money and the pursuit of fleeting happiness. She hates being who she is, feeling their hunger, feeling their need.

The water spirit's face moves, dipping inward, its way of showing a frown. "I have to go. The hungers awake. You need to stop them from going in. The hungers feed more and they demand more."

She stands up, her feeling of peace gone. In the distance, she knows the darkness waits for its meal.

Ah-ma looks as if she is sleeping, her face serene and still.

She can only stare at those ageless features, unable to cry. Nearby, the clan has assembled. Her mother, her aunts and uncles. They are not crying. They are after all a stoic family.

In her jeans pocket, the dragon-form dagger trembles. She pulls it out and looks at it. The green eyes are seeping water. Somewhere, her grandfather is crying.

"She's gone." Her mother places a gentle hand on her shoulder. "Gone to the Celestial Court to guard the Emperor. Be happy for her."

Somehow, she remembers happier times, her grandmother teaching her how to make dragonbeard candy.

Somehow, she remembers the patient voice of ah-ma, reciting the Lotus Sutra.

She holds up the dagger and the jade eyes drip tears.

I will not cry. I will not cry.

Yet, as she sits beside ah-ma's body, her fingers curled around the dagger, drawing strength from it. It will be a long night. Her aunts have already started burning paper money. The smoke swirls up like dancing tian lung. Perhaps, mother is right: ah-ma is gone to protect the Emperor.

Definitely changing colour.

She pats the streak of lighter hair, amused. It is a

coppery red and obvious to the naked eye. Her teachers will surely see it.

The smells of dinner drift along the corridor. Fried fish. Sizzling garlic. Sesame oil. The setting sun casts a golden sheen on the roof tops of the blocks of flats. It is the magical moment before night.

She inhales the aromas, glad to be alive.

A chill wind touches her skin.

Her dagger vibrates. She feels it through her bag.

A dark shadow darts away at the corner of her eye. It looks larger than the usual hungers she hunts at night. She gives chase, drawing her dagger. She passes by children who whisper gleefully: "Dragon, dragon, dragon."

This one is going to be tough.

Fire creeps up her arm.

She signs her name as Mica. Kim jokes about it. She ignores it. She is called Mica online, by the coven leaders and her coven-mates across the continents. Mica is her personal name, just as Yin Tian is the name used by her elders.

She has seen her dragon form. It glitters, just as mica glitters with light reflected. She is a ti lung and the name fits.

Mica Dragon-form.

The large hunger taunts her. It is also very aware, unlike the hungers who are just by-products of emotions.

Mica Dragon-form.

She refuses to rise to its baiting.

I have been waiting for this day to meet you, Sheng's

granddaughter.

She stiffens. This hunger knows her grandfather.

I want to feast on your life, little ti lung, Mica Dragon-form.

She visualizes her circle of protection and holds her dagger up. Salut. Always be polite to your enemy, Kim has said once. Wolves posture a lot, she counters back.

In her mind, the four dragons rage, straining to be unleashed. Her dragon-form bristles and bares teeth. Her scales flash like mica under the sun. She wants to fight this thing.

But I will make you dance for me. Wait. Pine. The battle will be soon. Not now.

"Stay and fight, hunger!" She shouts.

Mocking laughter answers her, then nothing –

The dark form dissipates in the breeze. She is left standing with her athame drawn and a gaping crowd of school kids. She shakes it off and walks away, pretending not to notice their giggles and pointing fingers.

It's my-kar, not me-kar.

Kim can be so sweet in a dorky, geeky way. She is still grappling with her feelings for him. He is now in the army. He insists calling her me-kar.

Mica Dragon-form.

The dark hunger knows her personal name. In magic, knowing true names and forms gives power. And control. Her mentors have taught her that important lesson.

But how did it know? How?

She is frightened. Her confidence is so easily shaken. Should she tell Mum and Dad?

Sleep is not easy. She ends up reading her textbooks, burying herself in schoolwork. Besides, her exams are coming.

Outside, the wind picks up, beating against the glass panels.

Perhaps, she will talk to the water spirit, check if there is something strange in the neighbourhood.

The water spirit is nowhere to be found. Mica stares at the still lake, apprehension sitting like a cold lump in her chest. Nearby children play ball.

The sun is warm on her back. Her sandaled feet crunch dry brown leaves. It is unusually hot and the trees are showing their thirst in their yellowing leaves and parched bark.

The hunger.

Worried that the hunger might have done something to the gentle water spirit, she starts to pace along the shore.

Enough!

This time, her ritual is more elaborate, calling her four dragons, naming them. The circle flares up with the dragon forms as silent sentinels, glaring balefully at any intruder. She pierces through the layers of reality…

…And what she sees shocks her.

The dark form shrieks towards her, its maw wide open as if to consume her in one single gulp.

Her entire body freezes. She tries to accept the truth that the hunger thirsting for her flesh is…was…the water spirit.

How did she get corrupted into such a...

Who did it?

Who corrupted her and twisted her being inside out, tearing out her goodness, her *everything?*

Mica has a bad feeling that she knows who the culprit is.

"Culprit" isn't exactly the word. Too gentle, too mild. More like "Murderer" or—

Her circle of protection surrounds her like a ring of sun-fire. This time, her dragon-form takes over, hissing and rearing like a striking snake.

The four dragons snarl and lash out with their talons. This time, they become her guardians, protecting her physical and spiritual body from harm.

"Dragon…"

Mica pushes away any feeling she has had for her former friend and meets the hunger head on, her dragon-form dagger singing in undiluted joy.

I am sorry, I am so sorry…

The exhaustion is crippling. She finds herself unable to get out of bed and go to school. Every bone in her body screams with pain and every nerve sharp threads of hot fire. Her mother peers in, worried.

"I made you some tonic soup," she says, shaking her head. Mica stirs, trying to answer her mother, and winces as her sudden movement triggers yet another cascade of pain. Her joints throb,

Is that the price she is paying for using the dragon-form dagger?

"You should go see Dr Tan about this." Her mother

sits down on her bed, resting delicately at the edge.

"Ugnh," Mica can only manage. Her head spins. Vertigo.

"Can you get up?"

"No," Mica whispers and she feels as if she is a newborn kitten mewing.

Beside her, the dragon-form dagger glows green.

Mica curls up under her blanket, shutting out the images of dragons on fire.

Ah-ma visits her in dream-time and nags at her about overtaxing her body. Then the dream dissolves into a spray of diamond-like water.

She emerges from the fevered dreams better and strengthened. Perhaps the tonic soups helped.

Standing takes some co-ordination. She curses limbs gone weak from lack of use. She manages to wear her school uniform without any major drama.

It is then she catches sight of herself at the mirror. The coppery streak seems to have grown more vivid, like the gold of the setting sun. She can't hide anymore.

She has to catch up with her homework which has piled up during her convalescence. She finds her marks plummeting. Her teachers sit her down and talk to her about her future.

"You have to work towards your goals," her English teacher, Mrs Peirera, says sternly. "You have so much potential, Yin Tian. You should get that re-dyed. Black." She glanced at the lock of hair, strands of gold peeping out.

What can a dragon-form witch do?

The darkness waits for her, a mysterious enemy who wants her blood.

In the dream, the darkness pursues her, laughing and mocking.

She flees the darkness, as if she is afraid of it.

In the dream, she fears the night, for it is the time the darkness awakes and begins its hunt.

When she wakes, bleary-eyed and heart-sick, she wonders who is the hunter and the hunted.

Mid-terms come and go. She finds her results dipping again. The principal, Mrs Tham, calls for an "interview". She dreads it. She fears that she might have to stop her duties.

Mother glares at her, daring her to say something.

"You are not a hero," Mother begins her barrage. "You are not your ah-ma. Stop it. We are no longer in the days of strife."

This cuts her straight into her heart. She feels the immediate flood of tears burning in her eyes. Does her own mother think it is all fun and games? Is she not worthy of taking over ah-ma's … ah ma's what – role? Rank?

No wonder the rest of the non-human groups think that the Lung, the Chinese dragons, are confusing. Aloof and reclusive; claiming to be protectors and watchers in their own right. They contradict them-selves.

She gives up wanting to argue with her mother and goes back to her room. She takes out the dragon-form dagger and places it gingerly on her study table. It gleams, its green eyes shining with its own light.

"You," she hisses at it, curbing the instinct to scream, balling her hands into fists. "I blame you. I *hate* you."

The dagger does not reply.

With a growl deep in her chest, her dragon part simmering like a hot spring, she ignores the dagger and walks away.

Have you lost the battle, little Mica?

The darkness laughs in the background, a dry rasping of leaves, rattling lungs and spite.

Have you? Have you?

No.

Fool Mica. Fool.

I will get you one day. One day.

NO ONE STAYS DEAD

Bracken Macleod

Tires screeching, the armoured truck thundered up the city street, ignoring traffic lights, barrelling around corners with just enough deceleration to keep from toppling over. Ray could hear the police sirens wailing outside. He couldn't see the cars escorting him, though. Not through the windowless steel walls of his mobile prison. The bench he sat on was unforgiving and cold and the chain between his collar and the floor was too short. Every bump in the road rattled his spine and, if he didn't hunch down to give the tether a little slack, painfully jerked his head forward. He'd asked his guards if the increased precautions were really necessary. They replied by attaching them with extra vigour. Despite moving on without him since his incarceration, it appeared the world was still plenty frightened of what he represented.

The costumed buffoons on the opposite bench sat staring at him with equal measures of loathing and fear on their half-masked faces. Ray was certain that, if given their druthers, they'd happily murder him. Damned be their heroic reputations and non-maleficent oaths. "Where are we going?" he asked.

Jurist opened his mouth to speak, but The Howling

held up a clawed finger to silence him. The Howling was a devilish red-skinned beast of a man, but he had a better sense of both fairness and mercy than the ironically-named Jurist, who was little more than a cripple factory. Hardly anyone he "judged" walked away from the encounter – or ever walked again for that matter. If Ray wanted to survive the ride, and do so in a way that didn't require a wheelchair, he was relying on The Howling's commitment to preserving his ever-diminishing humanity.

"Look fellas, I don't know why I'm being transferred, but my therapist says that I'm making real progress. I've got my compulsions under control, an inventory of restitution to make, and a commitment to getting better. I'm working on making amends. I mean, I will be once I'm allowed contact with the outside again. Moving me is just setting back my rehabilitation."

The Howling sneered, baring elongated canines. "How many times has Lamplight sent you to the Havens? How many times did you escape just to start over like nothing ever happened?" Death Ray *had* been in and out of The Havens Institute for the Criminally Insane like it had a revolving door. This time was different. If his last few months of freedom had been as productive as he'd desired, a remote chaos-contingency would have gone off after his incarceration, springing him like any other time he'd walked out of the asylum unrepentant, recalcitrant, and ready to pick up where he'd left off. But Lamplight had been hounding him so viciously during those weeks, Ray hadn't been able to plant a tomato stalk in the garden let alone explosives around the city, or a sleeper assassin in the government. He'd been cornered. And in a last desperate act, lashed out. His swan song as a super-villain had been petty and cruel and certainly not super in any way. That was what led to his latest residency at The Havens. The one during which he'd actually enjoyed the benefits of their attempts to fix what was broken in him.

"I know I've done terrible things, but I swear I'm on the mend. I don't even go by 'Death Ray' any more. Just plain old Ray. I'm a simple man with no higher ambitions than to be well."

"How many of your victims are well?" Jurist scowled and balled up his fists. He cleared his throat, but it didn't make his voice any less gravelly. That signature rasp was a gift from Death Ray.

Ray shifted, trying to keep the metal clamp around his neck from pinching the skin at base of his shaven skull. His back ached from being hunched over and the metal bench was making his ass numb. "You're on my list of reparations, incidentally. I've pledged to make amends to you, Subterranean, Ms Miracle – all of you." He felt a pang of remorse twist through his mind as he thought of Ms Miracle. *How do you make amends for something like that?*

Jurist made to stand up. Ray flinched, squinting his eyes and waiting for the lead-weighted knuckles to crush his cheekbone or shatter his jaw. Waiting for justice. When he didn't feel the hit he opened an eye to see The Howling whispering into Jurist's ear, a calming hand placed upon his shoulder. "It's his fuckin' fault!" Jurist protested. "Whatever he did, it's his fault and he's gotta be held to account."

"He'll pay his debt," The Howling said. "But first, we have to take him there. He's the only one who knows how to undo it."

"Undo what?" Ray asked. He struggled to find adequate words. "Name it. I'm ready to take it all back. Just tell me where you're taking me."

The Howling sighed. "We're taking you to see Lamplight."

Ray's stomach knotted and the noise in the truck dulled as fear overtook him, plugging his ears and quickening his pulse. He tried not to show how terrified he was. The look of near delight in Jurist's black-ringed eyes told him that he was doing a piss-poor job of it. He closed his eyes and went through one of the deep breathing exercises that Dr Meryl had him do when he got the urge to stab an orderly in the neck or set a nuclear device in the Brick City Stadium. Strangely enough, both compulsions were managed by the same simple mental exercise: imagine himself in the shoes of his victim.

Take a moment, Ray, and picture yourself sitting at a football match with your best friend or lover. Are you there? Good. Now picture yourself at the game and think about how it would feel if your best friend, let's say, was vaporised in front of you. How would that make you feel?

Empathy. He'd never felt any that he could recall. Born a perfect sociopath. Except, Dr Meryl had shown him that fact wasn't any truer than anything else he'd led the world to believe. As they worked together, he learned that he'd been born a perfectly normal person, with feelings just like any other. Through years of systematic torture he'd been *taught* to discount everything but his own feelings – to never feel anything but his own pleasure and need. The people who raised him had made him this way. It wasn't an excuse; it was an explanation.

And having been explained, she said, *we can work together to undo what they did to you. To make you better. Do you want to get better?*

I do, he thought. *But there are some things you can't undo.*

The truck turned another corner and while Jurist and The Howling struggled not to let centripetal force and their heavy armour slide them down the bench toward the back of the cabin, Ray's collar and chain kept him rooted to the spot. He imagined that if the vehicle crashed it'd be a lot like being hanged for his crimes. His neck would probably snap from the sudden jolt of his restraint and Jurist would get exactly what he wanted: retribution.

Ray took another deep breath and opened his eyes. His fear had lessened and he could speak again. The reality of what they'd said sunk in. "Lamplight? What do you want me to undo that Lamplight can't? What *can't* Lamplight do?"

Jurist's lips peeled back in a snarl and his jaw flexed as he clenched his gleaming white teeth. The Howling laid his hand back on his friend's shoulder and said, "He's had no contact with the outside world for over two years. He has no idea."

"No idea of what? Lamplight can fly and hold his breath for hours and punch through mountains. He's bulletproof and laser proof and immune to poison. Nothing can touch him. So what do you think I can fix that he can't?"

"You really hate him, don't you?" Jurist said.

"Hate him? No. I mean, once upon a time I did. But now, I … I guess I understand him."

"What do you understand?"

"I know why he does what he does. I know what makes him … Lamplight."

The Howling stood up in the cramped cabin and glowered down at Ray. He'd found the crimson man's soft spot. For every moment of struggle The Howling endured because of what he was, Lamplight was simply good by virtue of what he was. The Golden Demigod was the standard to which the red son of a demon held himself. He admired Lamplight – worshiped him like the beacon of hope that was his namesake. Ray looked away, staring down at the floor, not wanting to see the look of increasing desperation in The Howling's expression.

"We're almost there," Jurist said, checking the GPS in his bracer.

The truck made a final turn and slowed. It came to a stop and the doors flung open. Ray tried to shield his eyes against the sudden intrusion of blinding radiance. He almost wet himself, thinking Lamplight was waiting for payback, but it was just the late morning sun. A pair of cops in riot gear and electrified truncheons stood guard while Jurist unfastened the chain from the floor and reattached it to the shackles binding Ray's ankles. He hauled him up roughly and shoved Ray toward the door. He stumbled, but didn't fall. The guards reached up to help him down.

"Don't touch him!" The Howling bellowed, shaking the walls of the truck. "Nobody touches him. You don't know what he's capable of." Jurist shoved Ray out the back of the truck where he fell flat on his stomach on the pavement, undermining The Howling's warning but humiliating Ray sufficiently so no one noticed.

"Get up! Let's go."

Ray did his best to sublimate his pain and pushed up onto his hands and knees. He was hauled up to his feet like a little child and shoved forward again. He jogged up the street as best he could with a hobbling two foot length of chain between his ankles. The guards kept what they thought was a safe but effective distance away. Taser distance. Ray pursed his lips holding back a grin, a slight feeling of satisfaction at their discomfort around him warming his belly. He took a deep breath and pushed down the feeling.

Ray craned his neck back to get a good look at his surroundings. At first, everything was unfamiliar. The street sign read Landry Lane. Then, slowly, he began to recognise the place. It had been redesigned, rebuilt, and renamed, but enough of the old street remained that he was able to orient himself. The ghost of Economic Avenue shimmered just under the surface. The block was the site of the single most transformative event in his life. It was the block where he'd fought his final battle against the 'Light. More than earning his doctorate, more than communing with the Elder Intellect from the Hyades, even more than his wife's death, that final encounter with the World's Greatest Hero in this place had changed him.

It had set him on the path toward being a better man.

Like him, the street had been transformed. The buildings had been restored, a new skyscraper taking the place of the destroyed Alger Tower. Except for parallel double paths on either side, the street down the centre of the urban valley had been replaced by a beautiful greenbelt garden at the end of which stood a small plain stone monument ... and Lamplight. A warm breeze funnelled up the valley in which the park had been built, fluttering Lamplight's yellow cape. Otherwise, the man stood stone still, staring at the monument.

Ray felt a sharp sting in his conscience and stopped dead in his tracks. Jurist shoved him again with a hard palm in the centre of his back. "I don't want to..." Ray sputtered. "I can't..."

"Shut up and keep moving." The trio pressed on, finally reaching the end of the road where Lamplight hovered just above the ground staring down at the simply adorned marker that read,

ALEXA "LEXI" LANDRY
24 May 1991-13 October 2013
AWAY ON ASSIGNMENT

Nug and Yeb! They buried her here? Ray marvelled at

how many he had killed – poisoned, irradiated, drowned, and burned – and it was this one alone who left his greatest mark. In a single action, he'd changed the face of this block from cold concrete avarice to a viridian tribute to life and its beautiful fragility. He blinked to dispel the tears and silently meditated on a mantra that Dr Meryl had taught him to control his baser instincts.

I am an interdependent being upon whom the world has influence, who influences the world with his actions and attitudes. Nothing I do is without consequence. I am responsible for everything and everyone including myself.

Jurist scowled at the display.

"Undo it," The Howling growled.

"I … I can't bring back the dead."

"Not that." Jurist grabbed him roughly by the chin and the back of the head and forced him to look at Lamplight. "This!" The still man's golden hair fluttered in the breeze and his cape flitted softly like a bright flag. Other than that, Lamplight hovered motionless, not blinking, not appearing to breathe. Still as a weightless statue.

"What do you want from me?"

"Snap him out of it. Wake him up," Jurist shouted, shoving Ray's face up toward the catatonic hero.

The Howling said, "Lamplight hasn't moved from this spot – not a muscle – not in two years."

"Not since…"

"Since you murdered Lexi Landry!"

Ray closed his eyes and reminisced. In their last confrontation, the former Death Ray had lured

Lamplight to what was meant to be his certain doom. The street had been a bleak urban bottleneck where his nemesis would be hamstrung by his overarching concern for innocent life. Surrounding the Financial District with a lethal electro-containment moat, Ray had trapped the entire population of the neighbourhood on the street and in their offices. Making them all his hostages, his human force field. If Lamplight hurled his power-armoured foe into a building, he'd kill people. If he unleashed his atomic gaze or sonic bolts, he'd kill people. If he fought back at all he'd be responsible for killing hundreds or thousands of innocent people. Of course, it was easy for him to do something to save every last one of those people. He could kneel down and kiss Death Ray's boots. Despite his name, that day Death Ray only had it in mind to destroy one soul. After decades of defeat and a months-long campaign of unrelenting intimidation and terror, Death Ray had been driven to confront Lamplight. He had nothing else left.

But of course, laying down his own life never entered Lamplight's dim mind. Nothing had ever come close to touching him. He was invulnerable to everything. He was the symbol of strength and unbridled potency to which the world turned whenever it stood on the precipice of failure and destruction.

He was everything holding us back.

Instead of bending his knee to the gambit, Lamplight figured he'd found a way to destabilise Death Ray's mech-suit armour by listening to the echo vibrations bouncing back from his ultra-low frequency super-murmur. Not a deep thinker, he hadn't anti-cipated the planned counter-measure. By the time Lamplight realised what he'd done it was too late. And Death Ray lived up to his name, refocusing that sonar murmur into the foundation of Alger Tower at the end of the street – tearing it to the ground. Forcing Lamplight to indirectly break his one inviolable rule. Pushing him right up to the edge of his ability to restrain his rage.

Oh, how Lamplight had punished him for that. Torn the armour from his body, his fingers shredding unrendable Elementium Steel like paper. He husked Death Ray, ripping metal and flesh and breaking bone. And Ray had panicked. He'd pushed the demigod too far. Made him confront his only weakness and as Death Ray had promised no quarter, he received none. In a final act of blunt and anaemic desperation, he'd aimed the Desert Eagle fifty calibre hand gun concealed in his armour at his principal hostage and unleashed gas-propelled Hell.

Death Ray watched Lexi Landry collapse with a gaping hole where her heart had been and then saw nothing else but a yellow blur followed by blackness until he awoke in the hospital.

Born anew.

"They buried Landry where she fell and Lamplight has been waiting here ever since. He just hovers here staring at her grave. Never sleeping. Never eating. He doesn't do anything. No matter how bad it gets anywhere else."

Jurist laid a hand on Ray's shoulder. It wasn't an offensive gesture. It didn't hurt. His gloved hand rested on thin cotton prison garb stretched over skin and fragile bone and he didn't squeeze or push or try to force Ray to do anything other than feel the touch of another human being – and unlike Lamplight and The Howling and a whole host of other costumed vigilantes and villains alike, the two of them were just men underneath it all.

"Undo it. Wake him up. Give him the antidote, deactivate it, or say the words. Whatever. But bring him back. If you're really rehabilitated," he said, "you'll bring him back."

"You have no idea the trouble the planet has been in since he went … catatonic," the Howling said. Ray looked around at the lush green park surrounded by gleaming glass and steel towers that extended to Heaven and thought about the world. *If the rest of it has transformed like this… Like me…*

He tried to place his own hands over Jurist's but the chains held his arms down. Instead, he dropped his head and nodded gravely. "I think I can do it. But you and your partner need to step back."

"Not on your life!" the Howling said.

"The effects may be reversible but I need to trigger the failsafe. When I do that, I have no idea how it'll affect anyone else within range," he bluffed. "You can see what it has already done." Ray inclined his bowed head toward the frozen hero. "For just a minute of your lives you have to trust me." The two capes conferred with each other silently. Jurist let go of Ray's shoulder and took a step back. The Howling followed. Together they led the rest of the security team back to the entrance of the park.

Ray held no illusions about escaping. Shackled as he was, he couldn't run. He had no henchmen left free or alive to stage a rescue. The Howling could close the distance of the park in a second, long before Ray could even clear the grave site.

If all hope weren't lost, they never would have brought me out into the world. They never would have even let me out of solitary confinement. They never would have even thought of me again.

He had no intention of running. He wanted to do this.

Ray stepped up close to the brilliant yellow-clad figure. Although dimmed, Lamplight still shone with a luminescence born from the radiant energy of his body and Ray had to squint his eyes to get near enough to whisper in his ear.

"I know you can hear me, Kurt. I know what you're doing. I've studied meditation and techniques for focusing consciousness long enough that I can see you've gone deep into a place where you think you can wait this out. I know you're trying to outlast, ride some quantum moment that'll make a single second of your life – however long that is for something like you – stretch out to infinity while ours tick on by. You've seen days like this come and go in between temporal cataclysms and cosmic anomalies that reversed the deaths of men and women like Black Narcissus, Boneshaker, and Special Delivery. Hell, not even Jurist over there knows he used to be The Interrogator before he died and came back. But we do. We've been on both sides of a retroactive continuity crisis and we know that no one stays dead forever. Not among our peers, anyway." Ray pointed down at Landry's grave. He waited a second, feeling the heat pulse of Lamplight's luminescence intensify just a bit. It was as if he could feel the demigod's consciousness rising to meet him.

"Except people like Macabre's Aunt June, Subterranean's sidekick, Canary, and Jurist's parents." *People like my wife.* "They all stay dead because they're the ones who make us what we are. They're part of the narrative 'Big Plan.' Who would you be if you hadn't been exiled from your dimension to serve out the rest of your father's sentence after his execution?" Ray thought he saw the hero blink. He continued. "I know where you come from. I know everything there is to know about you and everyone like you. How else do you think I got us all to this point?"

The glowing man exhaled, long and slow.

"I've followed the quantum rabbit hole down to where it splits off into multiple realities. I've meditated on a hundred alternate worlds – places where you and I are brothers, lovers, where we are the same person. I've seen all the splits down a thousand different possible roads and I know where they all lead. Every last one of them ends up right here. The singular moment in infinite time where an unknowable number of possibilities converge at one incontrovertible fact: Lexi Landry is dead and she's never coming back. Not in a million billion realities. You can't rewrite the history of this one. This is the one place where nothing will ever change."

The hero clenched his fists.

"And that's why you can't move. You fear nothing because nothing can hurt you. Now the love of your life is gone and for the first time you're suffering like a real being and not just feeling the indifferent warmth of a sun god. Having never experienced pain before, I imagine it's unbearable. You've lived your whole life afraid of nothing. And here it is. A grave filled with the corpse of your lover, who is nothing and will never be anything again. You can't change it. You can't bear it."

Ray leaned so close into Lamplight's ear that the hero's white hot skin blistered his lips. "I killed her," he whispered. "I removed your only reason for being here. Go home, Kurt. Leave us and live your life and feel pain and love and be happy where you belong. You're too weak to stay here."

The demigod began to tremble and glow and swell. In an instant he grew into a white ball of energy that flung Ray back to the edge of the park. As quickly as it expanded, it collapsed with a thunderclap. The giant ball of white light shrank down to a pinpoint like a distant star and then snuffed out.

The cry from The Howling made the windows in the valley rattle. A few shattered, falling to earth in a stabbing rain. Jurist closed the distance and wrenched Ray up from where he'd fallen, throwing him back into the middle of the scorched and brown greenbelt.

The heroes fell upon him, fists pummelling and boots breaking his bones. Ray huddled up to protect his face and his organs against their onslaught.

"What have you done? What did you do?" Jurist screamed as he kicked.

"I won," Ray choked.

ACE IN THE HOLE

Mike Chinn

I froze as another trickle of dirt rattled somewhere near in the darkness. I strained my eyes, waiting for that first flicker that would tell me it had started.

There, maybe?

No. Just another trick played by over-imaginative nerves, and eyes that had already been seeing things for two hours. I slumped back into the corner of my cramped hiding place, pulling the stiff collar of my flying coat up around my ears, trying to sink deeper into the thick leather. God, but it was cold! Old gags aside, I'd never have believed it was going to be as bitter as this, past experiences notwithstanding.

I found my mind drifting back to The Palace, two thousand five hundred miles away in New York; to Leigh in her newest sequins, choreographing the waiters and customers with equal ease; to Franco hashing up something special in the kitchens. The cosy, warm kitchens.

And here I was: Damian Paladin, restaurateur to the Manhattan rich on my good days; and investigator of all the things that have no place in the heady world of High Society America, 1935. Crammed into a lightless, airless place in Seattle's suburbs, on a cold and damp November night – this wasn't a good day. I tried to shift my weight, to ease some of the creeping numbness growing happily in my butt, but only succeeded in hitting my head off the low roof.

"Happy Thanksgiving," I muttered sourly, once I'd used up all the colourful invective I knew. It was a pip, all right.

More dirt fell nearby, but this time I was sure I sensed some movement. Another handful of clods shifted grittily – and I knew something was moving out in the thick darkness. I heard a heavy dragging – as though all the worms this side of the Atlantic had chosen to take their vacation here. A hollow knock, a thud followed by more dragging; and then a pallid, cold glow began to sift through the total blackness – almost blinding eyes grown accustomed to the complete lack of light, despite its thin, phosphorescent quality.

Then I was no longer alone. Something the colour of dead maggots, oozing with corpse-light, dragged itself to within three feet of where I crouched – and halted, rearing up as much as it could in the confined space.

It had a strangely conical head, totally devoid of features, spreading out from thin shoulders like a dope-addict's dream of a tulip, and a scrawny torso that tapered off into the shadows. Arms that looked boneless, ending in huge, spade-shaped hands which scraped nervously on the plain, wooden floor. The smooth planes of the cone twitched this way and that, finally orientating themselves in my direction – and I didn't need the crawling in my gut to know that somehow it was watching me.

What? came a bubbling voice, a voice filled with mouldy clay – the seepings of stagnant ponds lost far underground. I couldn't tell if the sound actually issued from the pallid shape quivering in front of me, or just sounded in my head, but the source was all too obvious.

What are you?

I snapped open one of the holsters hung from my belt and felt the comforting weight of my Mauser as I pulled the automatic free. It was one of the *Schnellfeurer* models, able to loose off all twenty rounds in little more than a second. Totally inaccurate, and I guessed no use at all against the thing before me – but I've always been a traditionalist.

"Exactly what you see," I replied, doubting the thing could see at all. The fleshy cone bobbed in a peculiar, somehow disturbing motion.

No, came the disgusting voice. *There is something more...*

"And what about you," I butted in, keen to get the thing off the subject of yours truly. "What are you?"

Exactly what you see, echoed the glowing thing, shifting its position, digging trenches with its spatulate hands. Now it was my turn to shake my head.

"Uh-huh." I waved the Mauser at the thin torso and its pointed head. "My guess is, there's a damned sight more to you than meets the eye, scrawny."

The thing reared up suddenly and I tensed, sure it

was about to rush me, and a lipless, black gap suddenly split the cone almost from base to peak. A stench I defy anyone to describe belched out of that obscene blossom, followed by a wailing hiss that left my eardrums whistling in protest. With a flailing of the boneless arms the glowing shape began to slip back into the darkness, alternately retching stench and howls at me as it fled. But I'd been ready for that particular move since sundown. I launched myself across the cramped space and clung onto the retreating flesh as though it was my childhood love returned after a lifetime of celibacy.

Somehow I managed to keep hold of both automatic and the creature's disgusting skin, which squirmed and puckered against me. I felt myself dragged down an endless tunnel, filled with vengeful stones that must have done some hurt in their previous lives. In moments I was encased in a dense layer of mud and slime that smelled even worse than my unwilling guide; and I figured it too held a grudge – the way the stench continued to probe my battered nose.

I seemed to fall for an eternity, shaken like a doll that's been found by a bored terrier. Eventually the endless tunnel gave out and I was snapped loose of my disgusting hold by a none too gentle swat across the shoulders from one of the creature's shovel-like hands. I tumbled briefly before fetching up hard against a loose aggregation of gravel and earth strewn with little aesthetic regard across stale-smelling ground. Grateful that most of my limbs seemed to still be in place, and facing the right way, I got painfully to my feet, brushing vainly at the smelly coating that had turned me into a two-legged mudslide.

I was in a dimly lit cavern, dotted here and there by the crumbling remnants of buildings that looked as though they'd been in storage since the Chicago fire: storefronts and grit-covered sidewalks, hotels and offices. Some of them even managed to make it to the roof of the cave, though it was a struggle that had left them weak and tottering.

And everywhere I looked, the walls and ceiling of the cavern were punctured with black holes, like a negative sky at night.

"Old Seattle," I murmured, realising they were remnants of a great fire, the one of 1889 that had swept the town. Fires had been quite the fashion during the last decades of the nineteenth century. Only I couldn't figure where the light was coming from.

But it didn't take long for me to find out. Rounding one of the decaying corners, I came face to face with my monster's granddaddy; or to be exact, the rest of it. It was like some huge white slug, curled smugly in the centre of a burned-out square, emitting the corpse-light that was giving the cavern its thin illumination. A frill of tendrils blossomed grotesquely from one of its ends, each of the limbs ending in the tulip head and spatulate hands of the thing I had so rudely interrupted nearer ground level. Most of the tendrils were curled close to the body – like kittens snoozing close to mama – but the one I'd hitched a lift with, and a new friend, were swaying like disturbed cobras above the main bulk, conical heads swivelling insanely.

Who? came that gurgling voice again. *Who? Who?*

"You got owls down here, cuddles?" I said, returning my slime-covered Mauser to its holster. "Better take care, I hear they're partial to nice juicy worms."

A couple more of the squirming arms came to life and raised themselves into the airless gloom. *What are you?*

It was an odd sensation, hearing that one throatless voice seeming to come from four bobbing heads – but with no cavern-echo.

"Doesn't matter at this late stage," I replied, starting to walk towards the pale bulk, and slipping my hands into the pockets of my flying coat. "But I know what you are."

Half of the remaining tendrils awoke and waved mesmerically in the air before me. I paused, knowing that one of those limbs alone could finish this interview prematurely – by now I could count eleven of them, and they were starting to ooze up and down on their fantastically extensible arms, beginning a hypnotic dance. I couldn't afford to be distracted.

What am I?

"The Mayor of Seattle thinks you're a ghoul – or rather a whole pack of them since you began raiding fresh graves four months ago." Now the thing was talking again, I resumed edging forward but I continued to watch the weaving limbs. "He's nervous.

He couldn't find a pat answer as to how the corpses got snatched from underneath, for the newspapers – and he's up for re-election next year. It doesn't do to make a politician nervous. Or don't they have them where you come from?"

I have slept long. I must feed.

"Sure, I understand that. Why, we're both men of the world." I stopped, judging I was close enough. I noticed that all the heads were up now – eighteen spade-armed tentacles that could move like – I didn't know how fast they could move, hence the caution.

"But you see, a nervous politician is a desperate man; and desperate men will believe anything. Well, almost anything. Which is why he called me in. I deal with those anythings sane people never think about."

I do not care. I must feed.

"So you said, brother, so you said." I dug my hands deeper in my pockets making sure I had a good hold on what I'd been hiding in there. "But you've had your day, chum. You're washed up. I can't guess how long you've been asleep under the earth, and I don't care. This isn't your world anymore – if it ever was. You're finished!"

I tensed, sensing the moment was almost at hand. All eighteen limbs had stopped their weaving and I could see they were poised to strike; and being trapped in this museum exhibit, hacked half to pieces, was not how I'd planned to take my hard-earned rest.

At the very instant I keyed myself up, something black and gelid opened where the tendrils met, and stared at me. It wasn't good: an eye that ancient looking at me that hard – I felt it could see too much. So I acted.

"So long, turkey," I muttered, pulling the two parcels from my pockets.

I leapt back as far and as fast as I could the moment I pitched the two hessian bags at the eye nestled in that glistening white mass. The heads began to strike – but as suddenly started to writhe chaotically. They flopped open and closed, foetid air whistling out, smashing themselves against the ground, stretching at the vaulted ceiling, and crashing through already crumbling brickwork as the contents of the bags began to do its work. A deafening howl that reverberated inside my skull tore bloody furrows in my poor grey matter. I ran for the tunnel through which I'd been dragged, suddenly eager to be out of this place. If they ever wanted to take people on tours of underground Seattle, this cavern would have to be taken off the guide-map.

In its agonies, the squirming bulk thrashed its limbs against building and rock. Chunks of the ceiling were already breaking loose; I saw one smash into the oozing flesh and half-sink into the stuff that was already beginning to turn semi-liquid. It's amazing the effect several pounds of salt can have on a body.

Crude? Maybe, but like I said: I'm a traditionalist.

It took more hours than I like to think to crawl back up that slimy tunnel; and all the time I could hear the crashing destruction of the cavern, and the scream of the dying thing writhing in the centre of it. When I was about halfway up a sudden gust of stale air rushed up the tunnel from behind me, carrying a load of dust and a familiar stench. At the same time the screams that had been ripping apart my skull abruptly stopped. The rest of the climb was done in blessed silence.

Once back in my cramped hidey-hole, I emptied the whole clip from my Mauser into the lid, shattering the cheap wood into toothpicks. Pushing myself out and digging up through the loose soil was the easiest part of the evening – but I still didn't want to spend any more time than I had to in that cemetery.

It was too much like old times.

THREADBARE

Jan Edwards

The Tarot are old, furred at the corners, their faces worn and their once gilt edges scraped to beige from decades of shuffle and lay. The spread is a tough one; easy to read but a bastard to explain without sounding like the ides of March. Seven of Swords on top of the Devil. King of Swords. Ten of Swords. I flip over each card and stare at it in turn. What can I say? Divination -chill runs up my arms, raising goose flesh that I rub away from habit.

Angela leans forward to examine her future. She has *resting-bitch face*, hardening into petulance. "What do they mean, Helen?" she asks. "Swords are bad, aren't they?"

She seems primed for something hitting the fan, which makes it easier to say what needs to be said. "Change," I tell her. "And challenges. The Devil is lack of confidence in making decisions. The Seven is … uncertainty. Gossip. Spite. Betrayal. You need to watch your back. The King is a man of intellectual confidence and the Ten is an unexpected end to a project. An ending – one that you didn't expect."

The younger woman reaches across the table – puts her hand over mine – leans in close and whispers, "It's you causing all of this. I know you called him. You called Michael."

"I have no idea what you mean." *Shit! She's that Angela.* I lay the final card, scrunching my toes, tensing my gut, anything to prevent my hands from shaking. *The Tower: there you are, you little bastard. Full house in the all-out war on the Angela stakes. Couldn't happen to a better person.* "The Tower represents conflict. The tearing down of everything that surrounds you. Angela, you do know Tarot is about what may be and not what is to come? Whatever is seen here can change because free will has…"

"You screwed him. I heard you!"

I struggle to recall when I last spoke to Michael much less fucked him. "I've had nothing to do with him for months. Whoever you heard Michael talking with, it was *not* me."

"Bitch! I didn't come here to have you spout crap at me. All this is shit." She rises, pushes my hand back and sweeps the cards away in the same movement. "Not as much shit as you'll be getting if you don't keep away."

The cards tumble, scrambling into the shelter of table and chairs. I am on my knees to collect them almost before they finish falling, knowing my neglected rugs are ingrained with dust and grit and cat hair. When I hear the front door bang I sink back on my heels. One card lays propped against the table's pedestal leg. The Tower. I pick it up – frowning at the fresh fold across the diagonal, adding angles to its painted lightning. *Damn it. I'm sorry, Gran.* Her cards, as tradition dictates, were a gift – or to be more precise a bequest. They are ancient. Venerable. Now defiled.

Oliver Catwell unfurls sleek red-brown limbs and comes to rub against my cheek, chirping his cattish comforts.

Angela Bateman is obviously trouble in designer heels; she is known for it. I would never have agreed to the reading had I known who she was. If she'd beaten me around the head with a brick I could not feel more damaged. Stroking Oliver Catwell's ears for luck I scoop up the rest of the cards, almost missing the stray hiding in a fold of the rug. I tug it free, half expecting to stare Death in its bony face. But this is yet another sword and I feel if not relief then a sense of completion.

"*Le Trois*," I whisper. "Heartbreak. That figures."

Laying the rescued deck on the table, I cover it with its purple silk cloth and go to make tea. I would much prefer coffee, with a slug of brandy, but know it would keep me awake until dawn.

The stoneware mug, the one with the moulded dragon curled around the belly, is tactile, almost animate when filled with warm liquid. Wrapping both hands around it eases the "reading chills" and stops the anger shaking through me. Aggressive clients are nothing new but Angela's visit is about a lot more than Tarot. Whether the warning is from Angela herself or from Michael is not clear. It hardly matters – I could not feel more violated.

I wander into the workshop where the paying work is done. Two looms dominate the space and both are strung and weighted with commissioned pieces. I sit at the larger of them to check the pattern already emerging across the frame. A wall hanging of stylised flora and fauna in the medieval manner is a melange of merino wool and silk. My own preference is for a far less structured style. But a commission this size pays the rent for several months.

My feet ply the treadles, prompting beams to shunt back and forth. Their comforting clack-a-chunk is like a warm plaid falling across my shoulders and I work without conscious thought, allowing the rhythm to sooth ruffled calm. Retreating into that trance-like pleasure where only the coloured yarns and clacking beams hold any reality, Angela's ill-aimed venom is eradicated with the physicality of weaving. I think of Michael and what might have possessed him to hook up with "Miss Leopard Print and Jimmy Choo's", this Angela creature, with her red-rimmed, hunted eyes.

The beams sway to a halt and I prop my forearms on the cross bar to examine progress.

Flowers? (Pansies to be exact.) A chintzy confection complete with pink ribbon curled between them in a Victorian-posy motif. *Pansies are the blossoms of visions and projections,* I think. *Curious. And really, really, not the plan.*

The clock has crept around to three a.m. and I don't have the energy to unpick the weave, nor begin to wonder why I would have created this nonsensical piece of Victoriana.

Sleep. I need sleep. New day – new perspective.

~~~

My dreams have followed the same trail for days. Following the fox past the Greet Inn, that isn't there anymore, and along the Warwick Road toward Tyseley close to where Michael lives. A never-ending trudge through dark, rain soaked streets lined with petrol stations and windowless blocks of industry, fabricated from pallid, angular metal. Nobody walks with me, or even passes me by. No one ever does. Cars wash along the street, interspersed with buses and lorries that fill my nostrils with their soot and diesel stench. Their slipstreams tug me towards the kerb's edge, rush headlong to traverse this featureless concrete and tarmac hinterland, and reach the sparkling promise of the city centre. I leave the commercial sector behind me, stalking through parallel lines of Victorian terraces in red brick and pebbledash, weaving my way through a slalom of dumped armchairs and flaccid black bin bags, which rustle beneath the caresses of wind and rats. I am walking past his door. His windows, curtained and dark, show no hint of what might be inside. They never have, and I don't ever want to know – except tonight. Tonight is different. Tonight I step up the impossibly tall steps and lay my hand on the door. My fingers stretch out and bend at the knuckles. My nails morph into curved arcs of honed ivory that claw slowly down the face of the blue painted door, once – twice – three times. The fox barks from the street ahead, summoning me to follow, and together we walk into the night.

~~~

Tracey brings me coffee, kissing me lightly on the cheek and bends to examine the weave. She turns to look at me with confusion in her eyes.

"They're faces." She touches the uppermost flower.

"Michael Thurso. No doubt about it. And this one … is this Angela?"

She is right and it makes me twitch. "I should never have allowed that woman to cross the threshold."

"Why on earth did she want a reading from you in the first place?" Tracey asks. "Just to start a row?"

There is no answer. I gaze at the woven faces. My dreams have been filled with Michael for weeks. Michael the contradiction, filled with spiritual energy, yet cynical as hell. "It was her easy way in," is all I can say.

"Well, from what I've heard she's a total psycho. Keep the doors locked. I'm pulling a long shift tonight so I won't see you until much later, sweetie." Tracey drops a kiss on the back of my neck, caresses my head, strokes her thumb and forefinger around my ear from helix to lobe. I want to bury my face into her neck and let her make it all better – but she has to work and I have things to start; things to end.

The door closes behind her and I pull out my phone to select Michael.

"Helen," he murmurs, "I was just meaning to call you."

"If that would be before Angela got here? You're too late."

"Oh…"

I swivel round to face the weaving. Reaching out to tap the faces with rictus fingers, nails snagging strands like a harpist noodling at their strings – uncertain of what song will fit the mood. "'Oh'?" I said. "Is that it? Your latest screw just paid me a visit and all you can say is 'I was going to call'?"

"I didn't send her."

"Yet somehow she knew where to come." My fingers tighten, nails gripping slackened threads. "I'd never betray what I've seen in a reading."

His breath whispers across the phone and away into the silence.

"She doesn't know though, does she," I continue. More silence. "Can't you trust her?"

"I don't do trust, Hel. Not anymore." His voice is a husk, as though unused for far longer than the half minute since his last sentence.

"Yet you're screwing her."

"That's none of your business."

"No more than I am any of hers... Look, Michael. You and I? Big mistake. That was the past. This is now. Get over it."

"I am over it. I can do what I like and you can't judge me."

I hear his breathing harshen and I sigh. He has never accepted that our twelve-month marriage was one huge error of judgement. "Going to bed with someone isn't done for the sake of getting away with it," I tell him. "If you do it because you mean it, fine. If you don't mean it, why bother?"

The moment plunges into the abyss of a disconnected call. I place the phone face down, not wanting it to ring again.

Silk and wool strands straggle up from the surface of the tapestry where my nails snagged the wefts. Floral eyes, noses and mouths are obliterated by ragged holes that resemble cigarette burns – damage stabbing deep, baring the warps' pale tram lines running top to base.

I feel a brutal urge to bind their wounds, to heal them. Never mind that they hate me, that I hate them. My hands move beyond my will, plucking hair from my own head. Long brown strands, silken – slippery – glistening still with life as they slide into the bodkin's unwinking eye.

I tack and sew. Folding strands into place and securing them with stitches so fine they are barely visible to my naked eyes, grafting features into each flower face. My fingers are muscular pink spider-legs stalking across the material's tattered web of warp and weft but my mind, my eyes, my soul, are wandering.

Darkness creeps into the room and still I sew, pulling strand after strand from my temples, suturing each hank as it is torn from the root, faster and fumbling. Fingertips sore – scalp raw and bloodied. I feel no pain – all the while transferring viscous red to needle and fingertips and tapestry faces.

The waking trance finally relents. I am exhausted, my hands resting limp on my thighs, mouth dry and eyes stinging. My heart is erratic, breathing laboured. I fight down the panic and stagger into the next room to reveal my Tarot, frantic for the certainty they can bring me. I turn up three cards. Death and Judgement do little to calm me with their changes and retributions. But the Three of Cups are a salve – celebrations. All will be well.

I go to bed. It's wide and cold and I wish yet again that Tracey could change her shifts. Oliver Catwell is no substitute but when he snuggles into me I breathe in his dusty warmth, and sleep.

~~~

I am in a street. Not the same street as in the previous night's vision. The bright neons and goldfish bowl frontages are Ladypool Road's Balti Mile. Glimpsed interiors are painted in golds and reds and purples contrasting with snowy cloths. Cutlery glitters before empty velvet-backed chairs. Around me, cold rain patters onto the paving stones spotted with pale blots of long-discarded gum, and wastepaper whispers along the edges of the walls. I cup my hands against the window glass and peer into the depths. Tracey is there. She waves and I am sitting beside her. At the next table Michael and Angela scoop Jalfrezi with dough torn from pillow-sized naan. Michael reaches back to clasp Angela's head – and forces it forward into the steel balti dish. As the girl's struggles grow feeble, he laughs at me. When I step forward to stop him … I am in the workshop. The rear wall is missing, opening up to the night with rain lashing across the loom. I begin to weave but the clack-a-chunk is forfeited for squeak-a-clunk. Rust patters across the back of my hands. The shuttle sticks, flaking, shredding, cutting threads, slicing yarn, splitting hairs…

~~~

I sit up, rigid, panting, my face and neck and breasts are wet, but with sweat now – not rain. Oliver Catwell is glaring at me from the top of the dresser.

"Sorry Olly."

He opens his mouth wide to expose his pink throat

and yellowing teeth in a silent rebuke before he stalks away.

I roll off the mattress and move across the room to pull the curtains aside. Rain is slanting across the sickly orange spread of the streetlights and friend fox trots through. He pauses to look up. Our gazes lock briefly before he is melting into shadows without seeming to move and I wonder if I am truly awake.

A car pulls into the drive and Tracey is dashing for the front door.

~~~

Tracey is all concern. "What have you done to yourself?"

She sets a bowl of warm tea-tree tainted water beside me and pulls a wad of cotton wool from the pack, dipping it into the liquid and wiping my scabbing scalp with gentle strokes. Her other hand is clasped around the back of my neck to hold me steady and I flashback to the balti house with its naan bread and violence. I flinch away from her ministrations. I feel stretched – febrile – my skin taught and rough to the touch, the lines around my eyes and mouth deepened like vertical threads of my loom worn free of weave through the friction of stress.

"I needed fine thread..." I whisper, clouding my fear with mundanity.

She glances toward the loom, frowning at my red-stained repair. "Those waking dreams again?"

I can only nod.

"Oh sweetie. Is it Michael? You have to cut him loose." She gestures toward the ugly repair. "Getting rid of that would be good." She smiles reassurance and takes my hand. Our fingers interweave and the world feels clean.

I swivel around to face the loom and take up my stitch-pick, cutting one tiny thread at a time, deconstructing the night's work. A literal act, but I have to start somewhere.

Tracey carries on dabbing.

We finish together, gathering the detritus of swabs, scabs and scarified art and consign them to the embers of the log burner.

In bed Tracey pulls me close, spooning, her arms close around me, her breath warm against my right ear.

~~~

Guided by the fox, I am drifting back to Tyseley, past the furniture shop and left into Seeley Road. Darkness is interspersed by occasional halogen lamps which shine a false sense of security for passersby that never exist, when the cul-de-sac ends at an iron fence. The fox slips through flaking railings and vanishes into a waste land of scrubby trees beyond. There is a car, an old Volvo, its tail backed up to the fence. As I move closer the glow within is brightening, flaring, outlining the figures within. A man. A woman. Unmoving. Flickering luminescence highlights their features. Michael and Angela are staring at me. Flames caress their faces and still they sit. I cry out but can get no closer, watching their faces engulfed by flame, blackening, melting, distorting, collapsing into themselves – nose first and then eyes, lips, teeth. Imploding like the celluloid heads of the birthday-gift dolls that my brothers had tortured — fixing them to lighted candles, melting them from within, gaping holes dripping globs of plastic, until there is nothing left but blackened fragments attached to charred torsos.

~~~

I'm aware of sirens passing our window, projecting blue tongues of cold fire across the ceiling's white expanse. Tracey stirs to pull me closer still and nuzzles my hair. "You're cold," she murmurs, "and your hair smells of smoke."

BONES

Adrian Tchaikovsky

Between the scarf and the hood, hardly anything of Elantris' face was exposed and still he was breathing grit, every blink grinding the stinging particles into his eyes so that he thought he would go blind before they reached Dust Port.

"Is this a sandstorm?" he demanded of the man in the locust's forward saddle, leaning forwards to yell in his ear.

"Sandstorm'd strip your flesh from your bones!" The rider's amusement was plain. "First time in these parts, then?"

"Domina Hastella never wanted to visit before," Elantris yelled. The man's back was offering no insights. "Which means you found something?"

Their locust dipped and dived, some current of desert air slipping out from beneath its wings. For a moment the pair of them could only cling on and let the labouring insect regain its hold on the element.

The rider cursed the beast, swatting at its antennae for emphasis. "Found lots of things," he called back. "But yes." When not proving a surprisingly able locust -wrangler, the man in the forward saddle was an academic, a Beetle-kinden named Fordyce Gracer, a student of the buried past.

Elantris recalled waiting for Gracer in a shabby town of white-walled, flat-roofed buildings where south had been the desert, only the desert, like the edge of the world: vast, ground-down stretches of broken, rocky country standing barely proud of the sea of sand. If there was some habitable place on the far side of that barren ocean, nobody could swear to it. Even airships that had tried to brave the storms and the heat and the abrasive air had either come back in defeat or not at all. *Surely nothing of any value to man lies that way,* had been Elantris' only thought. And yet not true: here were Elantris and, on the locust ahead, his mistress Hastella, two Spider-kinden come all this way to inspect her family's investment.

"It didn't used to be like this," Gracer bellowed. He seemed to be guiding the locust lower, but the blowing sand kept Elantris from taking a look as he hunched in the Beetlekinden's wind-shadow.

"Like what?" he managed.

"We've known for a while this wasn't always a desert. Sea was much closer, and we've found where rivers were. It was green, all this."

"So what happened?" To Elantris it sounded like something out of the old stories, that some ill-worded curse could parch a whole country to this death-by-dust.

"Time happened," was Gracer's curt reply. "Things change. You go digging around the place as much as I have, you realize that. But in this case it's a good thing. When the desert came, it buried a lot of fascinating stuff, and that stuff's still there. So long as it's out of the wind, you'd be amazed what secrets the desert keeps."

Then the locust had spread its legs, although its wings flung so much sand up that Elantris could not even see the ground. A moment later the insect came to a clumsy, skidding stop, hopped a few paces as though uncertain, then folded its wings primly.

"Welcome to Dust Port!" Gracer boomed. "Dig's just a little way on. You'll learn to love it, just like we have!"

A moment later the wind lulled, the dust swirling and sinking, revealing a camp of tents and slope-sided shacks ringing a stand of stunted trees that Elantris thought must be a watering hole. Gracer was waving at a train of animals winding its way in from the far side, a half-dozen round-bodied beetles with ridged, black shells, laden with boxes and barrels but stepping lightly enough that he guessed the containers were empty. A little logic suggested that the caravan had been sent to Dust Port from the dig site for supplies.

Elantris dismounted and made it to the other locust just in time to help his mistress down. She was sufficiently swathed in silks that he had no clue to her mood, but then even her bareface was seldom a good guide to that. They were both Spider-kinden, but Hastella was pure Aristoi, a distant scion of the Aelvenita family that was paying for Gracer's research. Her Art always hid her true thoughts deep behind her mask of watchful patience.

So has he finally found something to repay the

investment? Elantris wondered. When Hastella had ordered him to arrange the journey she had not seemed keen, so much as resigned.

Elantris was just a poor secretary: letters, music and a little divination on the side. What would he know?

Gracer was heading off for the caravan. Beetles like him were tenacious, robust and found everywhere, just like the insects they drew their Art from. They got caught in Spiders' webs like any other prey, though, and now Gracer's little struggles had attracted the spinner's notice.

Hastella watched him go, then gestured imperiously for Elantris to follow her over to a ramshackle collection of wood that turned out to be something like a taverna. There, he procured some watered wine from the leathery-skinned Fly-kinden proprietor and brought it over hesitantly.

"It won't be much, Domina," he murmured. "I think it has sand in it."

She hooked her veil down so that he would receive the sharp edge of her expression. "If there's anything within ten miles that doesn't have 'sand in it', it's news to me." Still, she took the wine and downed it without a flinch, which was more than Elantris could manage.

He looked about the close slope-ceilinged confines of the taverna's single room, the stifling air glittering with dust motes where the sun crept in. There were a couple of big Scorpion-kinden sitting in one corner: waxy-skinned, bald men with snaggling underbites and claws on their hands. A scarred Spider woman reclined nearby, wearing armour of silk and chitin, and with a rapier displayed prominently at her belt. Most of the rest of what passed for the taproom was taken up by a dust-caked party of Flies and Beetles and a single sullen looking Ant-kinden, all glowering at Elantris when they caught him looking their way. In Dust Port you kept your curiosity to yourself.

"You think I'm mad, of course, to come out here," Hastella said softly.

He started guiltily. "I would never…"

"Gracer is quite the scholar, you know. He believes what he does is important. He's right, though perhaps not quite in the way he thinks."

"Mistress, forgive me, I don't even know what he does, what anyone could be doing out here."

"The past is a book, and knowledge is never wasted. A grand discovery, an ancient palace, a city from time before record lost to the sands, these things buy status and prestige for him as a scholar, for me as his patroness. For the Aelvenita as my kin. And sometimes men like Gracer turns up something genuinely intriguing – some scrap of ancient ritual that might be put to use, some antique blade still sharp despite the ages… Knowledge is never wasted. But, like good wine, it is sometimes best kept to those who appreciate it. After all, Master Gracer would scrabble in the earth with or without the patronage of the Aristoi. Better that we pay for his hobby, just in case it profits us. Just in case he finds something remarkable…"

"Mistress, can I ask … what was it drew you here,

really? You wouldn't say…"

"No, I would not. Not back where the foolish lips of a secretary could spread the word." Her cold look did not endure, seeing his hurt expression. "Very well, Elantris, as we've arrived." She reached into one of her many pouches and produced a folded paper. "Feast your eyes."

For a long time he stared at the sketch, turning it and turning it and trying to understand what he was looking at. In the end he was forced to confess his ignorance.

"It's a skull, Elantris. A drawing of a skull."

As though the sketch had been one of those trick images, abruptly he saw it, the line of the jaw, the eye socket, the teeth; he had never seen such teeth. "A skull of *what?*" he asked.

"That's just it," Hastella confirmed. "Nobody knows." Her gaze might have been fixed on some image that existed only in her mind, but Elantris fancied that, while he studied the sketch, she had been staring at the two Scorpion-kinden, and that they had been looking back, yellow eyes fixed narrowly on the Spider Arista. *Brigands?* was Elantris's alarmed thought. Scorpions hereabouts were not noted for their genteel or law-abiding ways.

Interrupting his thoughts, Gracer ducked in, spotted them and ambled over, managing a creditable bow before Hastella. "Domina, we're ready to head to the dig site. You may fly the last leg if you wish, but we have a howdah for you if you prefer a more comfortable ride on the beetles."

"So kind, Master Gracer, and I accept." She favoured him with one of her warmest smiles, the kind she reserved for truly useful underlings – and which Elantris himself saw precious few of.

~~~

Gracer's dig was out where the bones of the earth jagged from the dusty ground, tiers of barren, red-rock uplands rising higher and higher until they broke free of the abrading hand of the sand to form the true mountains that spiked the horizon. It was a stark, uninhabitable, malevolent country, and yet even here people lived. Riding atop one of the pack beetles, Elantris saw huddles of huts that must count as villages, corrals of animals.

"What did they raise here?" he asked Gracer.

"Crickets, beetles," the man explained. "The local varieties barely need to drink from one tenday to the next. The herders let them out before dawn, and their carapaces catch the dew like cups. If you know what you're doing you can fill your water-skin from them."

"And you say this place was once green!"

"Look ahead." Gracer's finger hands drew out landmarks from the stepped and broken terrain. "See the land dip there? Follow the gully up. That was a river once. People lived here, many people. This land wasn't just good enough to keep them alive, it was good enough to fight over."

"How do you know?"

The Beetle-kinden's teeth flashed in his dark face. "Because of what we found, young Spider. Because of what brought your mistress here."

Monster bones? But it was plain that Gracer meant more than that.

The dig itself was a large tent backed onto a sheer rock face, surrounded by a collection of smaller shelters, all dust-coloured, patched canvas looking as though it had suffered there for decades rather than just under a year. The motley collection of people who came out to greet them had rather the same look. Elantris's image of academics was the elegant and sophisticated, debating some point of abstract interest in an Arista's parlour, not this pack of weathered, villainous men and women, their hardwearing clothes layered with dirt and their hands calloused from the spade and the pick.

Gracer was making introductions, but the names passed Elantris by – even though he knew Hastella would recall every one. Instead he was just looking from face to face, wondering how one would separate a scholar from a fugitive killer just from the look. A half-dozen were Beetles like Gracer, stocky, dark and powerful, and there were a couple of Elantris's own kinden as well as three Flies and a lean Grasshopper woman employed to look after the locusts.

Elantris could see how such a team would function out here, the strengths each would bring. Every insect-kinden had its Art, the abilities it drew from its totem. The Flies would bring swift reflexes and the wings they could manifest on demand, able to scout the sands as swiftly as the saddled locusts. The Spiders drew on their archetype's patience and presence. The Beetles had their rugged endurance, and the

Grasshopper must own that most ancient of Arts, able to speak with her kinden's beasts. Elantris watched her commune with them before walking off to their pen with the great creatures trailing meekly behind her. Without Art the merely inhospitable would have become uninhabitable.

Art aside, the barren surroundings and the looming rock face oppressed Elantris, loaded with an invisible threat that plucked at the edge of his mind. He felt as though some predator was laired there, crouched within those cliffs having drawn the substance of the desert before it as a blind, to entrap the incautiously venturesome. He glanced at Hastella, but her smooth composure admitted nothing of her thoughts.

And besides, this was one reason she kept him at her side, despite his more general failings. He had good eyes for the invisible, and what was history if not a great edifice of the unseen?

I shall have harsh dreams here.

He came back to himself because Gracer was guiding his mistress towards the largest tent, and presumably she had invited him to show her his finds, or else he was just too enthusiastic for propriety. Elantris followed hurriedly, catching the Beetle-kinden's words.

"We've dug a selection of trenches, and we hit stone everywhere: foundations, loose blocks, all of it worn by the sand but still recognisable as the work of human hands. No idea how far it extends – that would take far more labour than we have – but I think at least several hundred inhabitants, potentially well over a thousand."

"Where are these trenches?" Hastella asked him.

"We've marked locations and recovered them, otherwise the sand will destroy anything we leave exposed. A day or so here and you'll feel the same way, Domina." A jovial chuckle.

"However, in here we've exposed the entryway to a dwelling set into the cliff. The entrance had been carved into the rock and then choked with sand and rubble, maybe actively filled in. People knew there was something here, though. We came here following travellers' tales."

"What did they say?" Elantris blurted out. Gracer and Hastella stared at him and he coloured. "About this place? What did they say?"

Gracer shrugged. "Some nonsense. They're not fond of it. Who would be? Nothing but dust here now – not like it was all those years ago. Thousands of years, Domina, five, ten... I've never seen anything like what we've found here – what we're still finding here. It's from before any history, from before even stories." And, with that, Gracer stepped into the largest tent, forcing his two guests to follow.

Inside, the heat was stifling, as though the very gloom radiated it. The slope of the ground within was steep where Gracer's team had dug down to the level of the old, that point in the sands that history had sunk to. There, the shapes of the past emerged from the dry substrate like ships from fog, and Elantris saw the angled lines of walls that had been ground down to mere stubs, the scatter of fallen blocks, carven sides effaced, worn almost smooth. At the far end of the tent, lit up by twin lamps, was a gateway, a crack in the rock that had been widened into a low rectangle of darkness, flanked by uneven, lumpy columns or, no... Elantris recognized the contours: statues cut into the stone. There the swell of hips, there elbows, shoulders. Time had played the headsman, though: barely even a stump of neck was left.

"We've collected a lot of odd artifacts, potsherds and the like, all unfamiliar styles," Gracer explained. "But you probably want to see the guardians."

There were a handful of pits dug there, covered with sheets against the dust that still got in, to hang in the air and prickle the throat and eyes. With a showman's flourish, Gracer drew the nearest one back, revealing—

For a moment Elantris was convinced he saw living flesh, movement, locking eyes with a fierce, ancestral glower, but there were only bones left of this ancient warrior. Bones, and the tools of his trade. An irregular lump of reddish corrosion was an axe-head, according to Gracer. A near-identical blot was a knife-blade. The armour had fared better, loose scales of chitin still scattered about the ribs, and curving pieces of some sort of helm placed reverently next to that yellowed skull.

"We've found more than twenty so far, buried before this gateway," Gracer explained. "Doubtless we've not found them all. Soldiers, guardians, sentries left to watch the threshold, interred with care and respect."

"What kinden?" Hastella asked him.

"Impossible to say." Gracer frowned, the dissatisfied academic. "You must know, from a skeleton alone the kinden is usually impossible to tell, unless Art has made modifications to the bone structure, like a Mantid's spines or a Scorpion-kinden's claws. The thing is, most of the old sites I've worked on, there's usually some fairly strong pictorial evidence to suggest who the locals were – statues of beetles, spider-web motifs, those mantis-armed idol things you get. Go back a couple of thousand years and that's usually the principal decorative motif. Here – nothing of the sort, not on the stones, not the walls – it all seems to predate that period entirely. Our dead friends here had some personal effects, and we've found a pendant with what might be a bee insignia, and a shield that's been embossed with fighting crickets, but it's circumstantial… Who were they? We don't know. We also found the remains of some dead insects close by, again apparently buried with full honours – two fighting beetles, a scorpion, but again, it doesn't necessarily follow that the people here were any kinden we know today. But you didn't come all the way to our humble hole in the ground to see these dead fellows, Domina."

"Show me," she told him sharply, reminding the Beetle-kinden of his station. Gracer bobbed, grinning, and headed for the doorway, snagging a lamp as he went and beckoning for them to follow.

Once inside, Hastella had gone still, so Elantris squirmed past, careful to avoid jostling her, and became so involved in proper decorum that he only saw the *thing* when he straightened up.

He let out a brief, strangled yelp and sat down hard, heart hammering as fast as beating wings. Gracer whooped, typical coarse Beetle, and even Hastella had a slight smile at his expense. Red-faced, Elantris picked himself up and backed away from the skeleton Gracer's people had assembled beyond the doorway.

They must have set this display up to impress the woman paying their wages. They had gone to some lengths to wire and strap the thing together, and had sunk bolts into that antique ceiling to suspend the thing. It was an impossible monster.

It was bones, just bones like the men outside, but no man this. It had been posed on its hind limbs, rearing up like a mantis, its forelegs – arms? – raised as if to strike down with their crescent claws. Its spine had been reconstructed into a sinuous curve, and Hastella's sketch had not done that head justice. Elantris looked up at it, that broad, heavy skull with jaws agape, baring its long, savage fangs.

The whole beast looked to be about the size of a man but ferocity dwelled in every bone of it, as though without the wire and the cord it would have lunged forwards to tear the throat out of any mere human.

"Is it a human of some unknown kinden, perhaps?" Hastella suggested, for there was little in the world that carried its bones on the inside, after all. There were humans, and there were a handful of species domesticated by them: goats, sheep. Nothing like this beast dwelled in the world any more, and for that Elantris was profoundly grateful.

"Probably not, Domina," Gracer told her. "The relative proportions of the limbs suggest that it went on all fours, and the skull... My anatomist tells me that it has a lot of attachment points for muscle – not a bite you'd want to get in the way of – but a far smaller brain-space than ours... It's something new, Domina."

"But this reconstruction, it's speculative," she offered.

"Ah, well, no." Gracer had that smug look universal to academics with the answers "The skeleton was found not quite in this, ah, dramatic pose, but still complete – tucked just around the doorframe. There wasn't much interpretation required. If you would wish to take it back, Domina, as a gift from us in appreciation for your support, it would make quite the conversation piece, perhaps?"

He was being too familiar again, but Hastella seemed content to let him get away with it. "Show me more," she directed.

The next chamber was a great, long hall, and for a moment Elantris had to stop, swaying, his eyes bustling with shadow movement that had not been cast by Gracer's lamp: hurried flight, the thrust of spears, a tide of furious darkness, the silhouettes of monsters. His ears rang with distant howls and screeches, hideous and alien.

He realized the hand on his shoulder was his mistress's, and bowed hurriedly. "Forgive me."

She was studying him, though, and he understood unhappily: *So, she brought me here for my eyes, then.* He had medicines for when the seeing dreams became too insistent, but if dreams were why Hastella wanted him here then he would have to forego the cure and suffer.

The floor was littered with stone, irregular forms that eventually resolved themselves into the broken fragments of statues. Once he had understood that, Elantris felt he progressed through a stone abattoir. Everywhere he looked there were broken arms, legs, sundered torsos.

"No heads," he said, before he could stop himself. The other two looked back at him.

"Very good," Gracer said. "Yes, this isn't just wear and tear, and our dead lads out there weren't just taking a nap. There's holes in some of the skulls and shields, broken bones. They died defending this place, I reckon, and whoever got in here, they weren't gentle with the fixtures. We guess this walk we're on was lined with these statues, and they all got knocked over, and someone took care to hack off every head and cart them off."

"But why?"

"Symbolic, probably." Gracer shrugged. "My best guess."

At the end of the hall was another low, rubble-choked entryway, and a handful of Gracer's people were working at it, shifting the stones and setting in wooden props. "Ceiling came down here," the Beetle explained. "And that *was* just time, I think. We're almost through, though. Seeing as you're here, I was going to get my crew to go all night, and maybe in the morning we'll all get to see what's in there.

No! The thought struck Elantris without warning. *I don't want to know.* But he said nothing. Of course he said nothing.

"A perfect idea, Master Gracer," Hastella said warmly. "So good to find a man of your profession who understands proper showmanship. Perhaps, after my tent has been pitched, you might join me for a little wine, and we can discuss what else I may be able to provide for you and your team."

Hastella's tent was a grand affair, overshadowing the little billets of the scholars. Elantris got a separate chamber to himself, metaphorically if not literally sleeping at the feet of his mistress. He had thought she would want him to wait on her while she and Gracer talked, but she had sent him off around dusk, and he understood why. It was not that she cared about privacy, but that she wanted him to dream.

The temperature had fallen as soon as the sun crossed the horizon, and yet the day's heat still seemed to linger feverishly in Elantris, leaving him alternately shivering and sweating, fighting with his hammock, staving off the night as long as he could while the murmur of Hastella and Gracer's voices washed over him like waves.

He was standing before that crude opening again, in his dreaming. In the dark of the desert he could not see the restored heads of the statues flanking it, but he felt their stone gaze upon him.

He did not want to go in, and for a moment he felt

that he did not have to, that he could still walk away and let the past keep its secrets. Then there was a rushing from all sides, and shadows were streaming past him, of men, of beasts, and he was carried helplessly with them.

He was racing down that hall, seeing the great flood of bladed darkness course on either side of him. He wanted to fight it, to resist it, but he could not: he was a part of it, it a part of him. He was responsible for what it did.

Ahead, the monster reared, bones at first but then clad in a ripple of fur and flesh. He saw those claws strike, the savage jaws bite down, flinging fragments of the dark on all sides. Then it was not a monster but a man in a monster's skin, face loud with loathing and hatred. There were many men, many monsters, creatures of the absurd, of the horrific: long-necked things with cleaving beaks; snarl-muzzled grey nightmares that coursed in seething packs; branch-horned, plunging things that used their antlers like lances. And the darkness was torn and savaged and brutalized by the monstrous host, but gathered itself and came again, pulling Elantris like a tide, forcing him into the jaws of the fiends to be torn and clawed and run through, over and over.

He awoke, crying and flailing and finally falling from his hammock completely – a real, physical pain to drag him from the morass of his nightmares. Looking up, he saw Hastella standing over him. How long had she been watching?

It was dawn already, the first threat of the desert

sun just clawing at the eastern horizon outside the tent. "Tell me," Hastella said, and he did, all he could remember, a jumbled, near-incoherent rant of a story, and yet she listened all through.

Gracer had been optimistic, and his ragged band was still trying to safely clear to the next chamber through most of that day, leaving Elantris nothing to do save kick his heels and steal bowls of wine when he thought Hastella was not looking. He wanted rid of this haunted place. Every instinct told him to cling to his ignorance.

At the last, close to dusk, Gracer came, with much apologetic scraping, to say that they were ready, now, to break through. The delay had plainly dented his confidence as, even as they passed down the hall of broken statues, he was insisting that they might find nothing of great import. Now the moment had come, he was abruptly nervous that he might run out of material.

His entire team were standing there, shovels and picks and props in hand. Elantris squinted through that dark straight-walled aperture, seeing that there was a space beyond it but nothing more.

Like looking into a grave.

As thoughts went, he could have wished for something more uplifting.

"Olisse, you go first with the lantern," Gracer told a Fly-kinden woman. She nodded curtly and hunched down, shining the lamp through. She was just a little thing, like all her kind, barely reaching Elantris's waist. If the ceiling ahead was unsafe her reflexes, and the Art of her wings, would give her a fair chance to get clear.

She slipped under the lintel, barely having to duck, and the darkness within flurried back from her. Elantris shuddered, remembering his dream.

There was a long moment of silence, in which they could see the light within waxing and waning as Olisse moved about. Then: "Chief, you'd better get in here," came the Fly's hushed voice.

"We're all coming in," Gracer decided.

"Chief—" Elantris heard the Fly say, but Gracer was already hunkering down to duck through the doorway, and Hastella was right on his heels.

"Founder's Mark!" Gracer swore, his voice almost reverent. The other scholars were staring at Elantris, plainly expecting him to follow his mistress. With no other choice, he scrabbled into the next chamber.

It was carpeted with bones. The chamber was wide and deep – deeper than the lantern would reveal, and everywhere was a chaos of ancient skeletons, heaped and strewn and utterly intermingled. Some were plainly human, whilst others – larger, heavier, stranger - must be the remains of more monsters, so that Elantris wondered if this had been some den of theirs, and these multitudes their victims back in the dawn of time.

We are well rid of such horrors.

Olisse was hovering overhead with the lantern, unwilling to touch down. Hastella was impassive, but Gracer regarded the ossuary with wide eyes.

"I never saw anything like this," he murmured.

By now Elantris had seen that, like the statues, one thing was missing. There were no skulls in all that chaos of jumbled bone, neither human nor other.

"How far back does this go?" Gracer was asking, and Olisse glided forwards, thrusting the lamp out, then letting out a startled curse. She had found an end to the slew of bones, and it was marked by a pile of skulls that reached close to the ceiling. The lamplight touched on the sockets of men and of fiends, the bared teeth of both united in decapitation and death.

What came here and did such a thing? Elantris wondered.

The contrast between the orderly burial of the guardians without and the mound of trophies within was jarring, and as much as he tried to convince himself that this could just be the respect that some ancient culture accorded its honoured dead, he could not make himself believe it.

"Well, obviously it's going to take a lot of study, to sort this out," muttered Gracer, the master of understatement. "It could have been … a number of things."

A massacre, say it, Elantris challenged the man silently. *A massacre of men. A massacre of monsters.*

The Fly came down gingerly beside that great monument of skulls that towered over her. Some of the inhuman relics there had fanged jaws great enough to seize her entire body.

Elantris thought he saw it in the lantern-light then, even as Hastella was turning to go. Beyond that mound of grisly prizes, against the back of the cave wall: more skeletons, human skeletons, still intact and huddled together, and all of them as small as a Fly-kinden. Or a child.

Then his mistress was heading back for the surface, and he was hurrying after her, out into the gathering dusk.

She would not talk to him all evening, nor to Gracer; just sat in her tent and, perhaps, tried to come to terms with what she had seen. The scholars were uncertain what this meant. Gracer dragged Elantris off to their fire and plied him with questions he could not answer, angling for some insight into Hastella's mind. Elantris drank their wine and bore their inquisition because it kept him from sleep.

Even after the scholars had turned in, cramming themselves into their threadbare little tents, he loitered on, in the steadily deepening cold, staring at the canvas that hid that fatal doorway, mute witness to an atrocity ten thousand years old.

At the last, it was either drop on the chill sands or haul himself to his curtained-off corner of tent. When he had finally opted for the latter he found Hastella still awake, staring at him as he entered. He could never read her eyes, even at the best of times. These were not the best of times.

In his dream the darkness was receding like a tide, leaving only bones in its wake. The monsters were all dead now, and so were the men who had stood by them. In his dream he watched each of their skeletons hauled up, clothed briefly in flesh in the moment that the blade came down, in the moment that the scissoring mandibles cut, then the head was free and the body was left where it fell. He was in amongst the darkness. The weight in his hands was the great head of a monster torn from its body by savage pincers, its mighty jaws gaping impotently, teeth helpless in the face of history. He placed it with the others, on that gathering pile, and did his best not to look beyond.

In his dream he retreated down that hall and smashed the statues one by one, taking from those carven human shoulders the heads of monsters, the gods of a vanished people.

In his dream, he moved the stones to wall in that doorway in the cliff, blocking up his ears to the shrill cries of those they had left alive within. In his dream it was necessary. He had cast his lot, given his allegiance, and that made them his enemies in a war that only utter extermination could bring to a close.

In his dream he buried his comrades and their beasts, those who had fallen in bringing this final conclusion to an ancient rivalry. He heaped earth on the shattered wing cases of beetles, the broken legs of spiders, the serrated mouthparts, the snapped antennae of those who had brought survival and victory to his ancestors.

He started from his vision to hear Hastella re-entering the tent, wondering blearily what she could have been doing. Had she been into the dig site again? Had she stood, staring mesmerised at that great trove of the fallen and the dismembered? Had she pieced together some story in her head to account for it all, and would that story resemble his dream?

She was a hard woman, honed like a knife by the politics of the Spiderlands, where to be weak was to fall, where emotion was leashed and used, and ran free only behind closed doors. Had she been shedding tears over that host of the unknowable dead? Had she been drinking in the tragedy of ages?

He thought not. A humble secretary he, but he knew her too well.

In the first grey of pre-dawn she had orders for Gracer. "I want all your team working double time in the new chamber," she told him. "I want a catalogue of everything you've found. This is the greatest historical discovery of our age, Master Gracer. You have two days to conduct an overview and provide me with a report I can take back with me."

Was it academic prestige or financial reward that glittered in the eyes of Fordyce Gracer? In any event he had his complement on the move before the sun cleared the horizon, filing into that darkness with their tools and their sketchboards and their lanterns, eagerly tossing theories back and forth.

Hastella watched them go with a proprietary air, standing under the canvas of the tent that shadowed the doorway. "Elantris," she said, when the last of them had gone in, "pack my possessions. We leave shortly."

He glanced at her, then at the gaping socket of the opening. "Mistress?"

Her expression did not invite further inquiry.

As he stepped out into the sun he saw that the camp had visitors.

A couple of the scholars had stayed at the fire, preparing food. They were dead – and soundlessly – before Elantris came out, and the newcomers were already heading his way. They were Scorpion-kinden, almost a score of them: huge, pale men and women in piecemeal armour, bearing spears and longhafted axes, and with curving claws arching over their forefingers and thumbs. With them were a handful of their beasts, scuttling purposefully beside them, slung low to the ground beneath overarching stingers and raised claws, each held in tight control by a leash of Art.

The brigands from Dust Port! Elantris thought, stumbling back into the tent. "Mistress!" he got out.

"I gave you an instruction," she snapped at him. "Go to it."

The light went almost entirely as a bulky figure shouldered in behind him, a Scorpion-kinden man fully seven feet tall. His eyes sought out Hastella.

"Go about your work," she said quietly. For a moment Elantris thought she meant him, but the Scorpion was loping past them both, heading for that shadowed entrance, and his men and his animals were on his heels.

"I don't understand," Elantris heard himself say.

"I think you do," Hastella said softly. "I think you have seen something of the past here, what was done of necessity by those who came before us. We are the Kinden, Elantris. We are the inheritors of the world, and that is the order of things. There is no sense confusing the academics with what might have been, or confounding them with what price we might have paid to ensure our survival. Such knowledge is not to be showered on the common herd."

"You knew…" Elantris whispered.

"Of course. Do you think this is the first such site? But such study is best undertaken covertly. Where men like Gracer are involved, there is only one way to guarantee secrecy."

There was a cry of alarm from within the cave, and then the screaming began. Elantris was trembling, staring into the beautiful, composed face of his mistress. She smiled slowly.

"I should have them kill you as well, I suppose, but you are a useful little tool, and I think I am fond of you. Now go and pack my bags, I'll have the mercenaries strike our tent."

He did so, numbly and, when he returned, the Scorpions were standing around Hastella respectfully – all so much bigger than she, and yet she dwarfed them with her presence and her Art, always the centre of her own web.

"I will send those I trust to further examine the site," she explained. "For now, block up this door. Let us seal away the monsters once again."

Too late, Elantris thought, watching them all, reliving the moments of his dream. *We are already outside.*

THE RETURN OF BOY JUSTICE

Peter Atkins

Nearly gave him a fucking heart attack.

Out of nowhere, like a machine-gun, bam-bam-bam -bam-bam on the door of Alderton's seventh floor apartment.

Jesus Christ, what now? Seventy-eight years old. You'd think he could watch *America's Got Talent* in peace without some asshole rapping on his door like the whole damn building was on fire.

In theory, people weren't supposed to be able to surprise the tenants at their own apartment doors – needed to be buzzed in via the street door's intercom system – but the theory didn't allow for the fact that at least half the tenants were dicks, regularly wedging the street door open so as not to inconvenience their fucking drug dealers.

Bam-bam-bam-bam-bam.

Enough already. "Not interested!" Alderton shouted, but the rapping just increased in urgency at the sound of his voice and he cursed himself for showing signs of life.

He levered himself out of the armchair and grabbed his walking stick to help him across the room. If this was another Jehovah's fucking Witness he'd tell them precisely where they could shove their *Watchtower* subscription. Reaching the door, he leant his weight on the walking stick – he'd need leverage if he had to slam the door against some mugger working the early shift – and opened up.

No mugger. No soldier of God. A kid, breathless and wide-eyed, black and maybe ten years old, who, the second the door was open, stepped into the apartment. Or tried to, till Alderton's walking stick pressed against his tiny chest and held him back.

"Whoa," Alderton said. "Where the hell you think you're going?"

"You gotta let me in," the kid said, part plaintive, part demanding. "They're coming for me. You have to save me."

"What?" Alderton said, and leaned his head over the boy to take a look up and down the corridor. "There's nobody coming, kid. Run off home. I'm all out of Halloween candy."

"Huh?" the kid said, mask of panic giving way briefly to a look somewhere between pity and contempt. "Halloween's not for three months."

Was that right? Jesus. He'd thought it was only a month or so since the last one. Older you get, faster it goes. Time runs fleet-foot to the grave, he thought, the picture of the sixth-grade school-room in which he'd first heard that line nearly seventy years ago clearer in his head than anything he'd seen in the last decade: Mrs Mitchell in her powder-blue blouse, reading glasses hanging from her neck by the vanity-free twine with which she'd replaced the broken gold chain; Susan Johannson, floral print long faded on her hand-me-down dress but already a heartbreaker, rolling a pencil up and down the slope of her desk by the flicking of a restless forefinger; Paul Worrall, gazing out the window and urging on recess, the sleeve of his green cambric shirt interrupted by the tight black armband for his Ranger brother, dead at Anzio.

"Hey!" the kid said, reclaiming Alderton's attention. "Help me. Please. They're going to kill me."

"Kill you?" Alderton said. "Don't be so fucking dramatic." Once upon a time he'd have bitten his tongue off, language like that in front of a kid, but he'd watched the neighbourhood go slowly to hell for the last twenty years and knew that nobody gave a shit about stuff like that anymore.

"I'm serious," the kid said. "I saw them do the other guy back of Pickwick's. And they saw me."

"Pickwick's?" Alderton said. "What the hell were you doing skulking around behind a bar?"

"So not relevant," the kid said, all but rolling his eyes, weary at old people stupidity. Alderton didn't know whether to laugh or smack him upside his little wiseass head.

"Why'd you come here?" Alderton said.

But the kid was done with backstory. "Help me," he said, his voice flat and small. "I'm scared."

Shit. Alderton looked up and down the corridor again. Still empty. The elevator was silent, too, and nor was there any sound of someone rushing up the stairs. But the kid's face was convincing in its lack of pantomime distress, in its stillness and surrender.

"Come in," Alderton said, ushering the kid past him with a hand between his shoulder blades. "I guess I can call the police."

"No! Not the police," the kid said, spinning to face Alderton as he closed his door. "You." And then, like it would help clinch the deal, "You helped me last time."

Last time? Alderton looked more closely at the kid's face, tried to place it. Seeing him in the context of Alderton's own apartment, the framed one-sheets on the wall behind him, helped for some reason. The kid gave his best shot at a smile, which helped more, and something clicked into place in Alderton's memory.

"Last time all you wanted was a damn autograph," he said.

~~~

It had been a year or more ago, and the kid had been accompanied by his stepmother, or at least a white woman Alderton assumed to be his stepmother. A joyless stick of a thing who hadn't had a lot to say through their twenty-minute visit.

The kid was a talker, though. Savvy little fucker, precocious and smart. Soon as they walked in, he glanced around at the shithole Alderton called home and said, "They hadn't invented residuals back when you were working, huh?"

"Kid, they'd barely discovered fire," Alderton said, and wasted a wink on the mother, whose returned smile was that of someone who'd learned to imitate social responses without ever quite understanding or approving of them.

Meanwhile, the kid had already registered the paused VCR image on Alderton's TV.

"Hey!" he said. "*Jeopardy*. The one you're on. Fast forward."

Alderton, surprised and a little creeped out that the kid could be enough of an obsessive to recognise a specific episode of a daily quiz show from a freeze-frame of the host, made no move to the remote, so the kid grabbed it himself – had to be the only person his age who even knew what a VCR was anymore – and zapped through to where one of the contestants picked the $800 square in a category called "Who Was That Masked Man?"

"You watch this every day?" the woman said to Alderton. Well, those were the words she used. Her tone, and the unfriendly twinkle in her eye, made it clear that what she was actually saying was Christ, you are so fucking into yourself.

"No," Alderton said, intending an explanation that it was only their earlier phone call requesting this visit that had made him find the tape, but the kid shushed them before he could get it out.

"Here it comes," the kid said.

On the screen, a much younger Alex Trebek said, "Justice was child's play for this actor who portrayed the teenage sidekick of TV's vigilante hero The Blue Valentine," and Alderton felt the same stab of humiliation he always felt when not one of the three contestants buzzed in.

The kid gave a groan of disgust. "Morons," he said, and stabbed the pause button before Trebek could shake his head at the contestants and say, "No-one remembers Chucky Alderton?"

Christ, Alderton barely remembered him. Hadn't been Chucky for decades. Charles G Alderton was the name on the social security checks that were all that kept him from skid row, and he'd been Charles, not Chucky, in the handful of B-movies in which he'd appeared in the late fifties and early sixties, back before he and the public had quietly agreed that they should see other people.

But the kid, unbelievably, did remember. Remembered not only the Blue Valentine's sidekick, Boy Justice, but also the actor who'd played him for the show's single season from the fall of fifty-one through the spring of fifty-two. Hence the phone call and Alderton's bemused agreement that the kid could come by and get some stuff signed.

Alderton had met fans before, even done a couple of in-person appearances at conventions organised by dealers in pulp fiction nostalgia, but this kid was different. For a start, he wasn't fat, white, and fifty – Christ alone knew how he'd ever discovered the show in the first place – but he also seemed alarmingly unclear about the lines of demarcation between TV heroes and the actors who portrayed them; Alderton had the not entirely comfortable impression that the kid believed he was visiting what was left of Boy Justice as much as what was left of Chucky Alderton.

But he was chatty and enthusiastic, loved action

movies as much as Alderton did, and really knew his shit – they'd got into quite the smackdown about which Bond was best – and Alderton had happily scribbled his name on several Boy Justice items for him: grey market DVDs of the show, an ex-library copy of *The Encyclopaedia of Pop Culture* (Boy Justice merited a five-line entry which managed to get two details of his costume wrong), and three – plainly very precious to the kid – actual pulp magazines from the thirties.

Not that Boy Justice had even appeared in the pulps. In the pages of *Strange Thrills*, The Blue Valentine had been strictly a one-man judge, jury, and executioner – a masked vigilante so merciless he made The Shadow and The Spider look like bleeding-heart liberals – and it was only the insistent whim of a TV executive that had given him a teenage sidekick for his small-screen rebirth and granted Alderton what little enduring fame he had. Thirty-nine episodes, the last thirteen (filmed after a summer break) less popular with the fans because Alderton's voice had broken and he was suddenly as tall as Brooks Barrett, the handsome piece of wood who incarnated the Valentine himself.

~~~

And now the kid was back in Alderton's apartment, and apparently in trouble.

"Come on, sit down," Alderton said. "Catch your breath. You want some coffee?" Oh, wait. Ten. "Can you drink coffee?"

"We won't have time," the kid said.

"Won't have time?"

"Here," the kid said. "You'll need this." He pulled something from his pocket and pressed it into Alderton's palm.

It was a souvenir pin, a cheap tin premium Alderton vaguely remembered them giving away in cereal boxes sometime back before the space age. Alderton's younger face, masked and smiling, with his own name lettered below and Boy Justice's name lettered above.

"Put it on," the kid said.

"This thing's probably worth money," Alderton said. "You should keep it, shove it up on eBay."

"Put it on!"

"Jesus Christ, relax already," Alderton said, sticking the stupid thing onto his shirt. "There. It's on. Now calm down. They weren't right behind you, so they're not going to know to look here."

"They'll have looked you up," the kid said.

"Looked me up?"

The kid pulled a cell phone from the pocket of his jeans and waggled it at Alderton. "Hello?" he said, in his best earth-to-idiot voice. "Twenty-first century. Apps. IMDB. Street Directory."

"You're missing the point," Alderton said, trying to keep the right-back-atcha exasperation out of his voice. Ten years old, cut him some slack. "What would they be looking up to start with?"

"Boy Justice," the kid said, like it was obvious. "I told them you'd protect me."

"Jesus Christ, kid! You couldn't just fucking run?"

"I was running," the kid said. "Shouted it back at them. Thought it might stop them." Not even sheepish. Like he still thought that.

"You're completely delusional," Alderton said. "You need to be on some serious fucking medication, swear to God. What the hell do you think's going to happen if they show up here?"

The kid shrugged. "You'll protect me," he said.

And it was exactly then – with the kind of timing Alderton had thought possible only on his ridiculous TV show – that his apartment door was kicked in and everything became suddenly and alarmingly real.

~~~

There were two of them, and the one who came in first was holding a gun. Not pointing it at anyone, just letting everyone know it was available should circumstance require.

"Look out, he's got a gun," he said conversationally, waving the piece around a little in case they'd failed to spot it.

While his partner did a poor job of closing the broken apartment door and the kid ran instinctively behind Alderton to huddle into a protective crouch on the La-Z-Boy, the one with the gun strode further into the room, checking it out briefly and dismissively before settling his gaze on Alderton.

He sniffed twice, theatrically, as his partner ambled up to join him. "Hey," he said, as if to an invisible audience. "Old guy smell. It is real."

Little prick. Alderton would have told him as much but he was too busy being afraid. They were little more than kids themselves – maybe twenty, maybe not even – and it was only as Alderton took in their polyester tracksuits and sneakers that he realised he'd been expecting pinstripes and fedoras, been expecting stock hoods from his fucking show. One would have been called Lefty and the other would have been called something Italian. You know, to add authenticity.

But the one with the mouth was unmistakably Irish, and his shaved-head partner was who-the-fuck -knew. Iron Curtain escapee, it looked like. Armenian? Russian? Some thug too dumb to pass the KGB entrance exam exploring the free-market opportunities of the new world?

"You must be Boy Justice," Irish said, the grin mocking, the tone contemptuous. "Some kind of superhero? Some kind of Dark Knight shit?"

"I'd've been Robin, at best," Alderton said. "But no, I wasn't any kind of hero. I was an actor." He knew that this wasn't news to Irish, that the bastard was just fucking with him, but still his hand gestured pathetically at the one-sheets on his wall as if to offer proof, like this little thug gave a crap.

Irish looked at the posters briefly, then back at Alderton. "Glad we got that straightened out," he said. "I was all set to shit my pants."

As if to point up just how very far from frightening he found Alderton to be, he tucked the gun into the tracksuit's waistband at the small of his back, and then displayed his empty hands, palms out, at his sides. Smiled, too. All friends here.

Reasonable men capable of coming to a reasonable understanding.

"Look, Pops," he said, "if you play smart, we can get this done without ruining the rest of your retirement. All you gotta do is convince me you're someone who knows when to keep his fucking mouth shut and we'll be out of your hair." He threw an insolent glance at Alderton's balding head. "No offense," he added, and tossed a grin at KGB, who gave an unpleasant bark in response that Alderton figured was meant to be laughter.

"What about him?" Alderton said, gesturing behind him.

"Who, the kid?" Irish said. "We'll be taking the kid." Thing is, he didn't use the word *kid*.

"What did you call him?" Alderton said.

"Huh?" Irish said, cocking his head a little, as if mildly surprised at anything even resembling a challenge.

"The kid," Alderton said. "What did you call him?"

Irish said it again. Conversational. Like the word was nothing. Like the kid was nothing.

"Watch your damn mouth," Alderton said.

His voice wasn't as steady as he'd have liked it to be, but still he felt the air suck out of the room and everything come to a bright and trembling focus as Irish took a step nearer to him.

"Watch my mouth?" Irish said. "Watch my mouth? Why don't you watch it for me? Watch it bite your fucking face off."

He snapped his teeth together, jutting his head

forward, and grinned with satisfaction as Alderton flinched and took a step backwards, wobbling and having to steady himself with his stick. He'd all but bumped into the La-Z-Boy, from where the kid's frightened breath was for the moment the loudest thing in the room.

"I'm not going to let you take him," Alderton said.

Irish cupped a hand to his ear and leant his head forward. "One more time?" he said.

"You're not taking him anywhere," Alderton said. "I'm not going to let you."

"Well, well," Irish said, smiling like he was delighted with the way this was going. He turned to KGB, made sure he was getting this. "Look what we got here," he said. "A Mexican standoff."

KGB looked around the room, as if checking. "No Mexicans," he said.

"No standoff," said Irish, and smashed Alderton in the face with a tight little fist that drove him to the floor and dropped him into blackness.

~~~

The basement door's padlock had opened easily once Boy Justice had selected the right size pick from his utility belt's collection, despite the strangely thick oil that coated the lock and made his fingers' work slippery.

Now, as he stepped cautiously over the threshold into what lay beyond, the young crime-fighter wondered, with a brief thrill of alarm, if he had in fact stepped over the very threshold of time itself. For the room in which Boy Justice found himself was no simple basement, but more akin to some terrible medieval dungeon!

Great vaulted arches seemed to lead into infinite shadowed spaces beyond this first chamber in which he stood, and said chamber was lit only by a dozen flaming torches – torches which illuminated a huddled body lying on its cold stone floor.

Glancing around with care to ensure that the motionless figure was indeed his sole companion in this eerie place, Boy Justice then crossed the room determinedly to uncover the mystery of this latest example of the evil workings of the Scarlet Claw and his minions.

Kneeling, he turned the prone figure over so that the flaming torches of the dank dungeon could illuminate its face – and a cry of anguish erupted from the youngster's throat!

"No!" he cried. "It can't be!"

The pale and lifeless face was one he knew all too well. The figure lying motionless on the dungeon floor, its blue domino mask removed by whoever had done this terrible deed, was none other than Valentine Dyson himself.

The Blue Valentine was dead!

Boy Justice stared with profound horror at the charred edges of the bullet-hole in the breast pocket of the Valentine's midnight-blue suit, still reluctant to believe the evidence of his own eyes.

Suddenly, evil laughter rang out as if from everywhere, echoing off the dank walls of the basement dungeon and, as if from some unseen control device, all the torches extinguished themselves at once, plunging Boy Justice into blackness!

The youthful hero leaped to his feet, readying himself for whatever new horrors the vicious crime-lord had planned for him.

Was that a movement behind him? A sudden movement, as of something rising from the shadows? Boy Justice spun around, fists raised and ready despite the all-encompassing darkness in which he was contained.

"Do your worst!" he shouted defiantly. "I'll go down fighting!"

"That's the spirit," a voice said from the black void. "But let us hope it shan't be necessary."

That voice! Was it? Could it be? Boy Justice held his breath, afraid to hope, until a match was struck in the blackness revealing someone he had not hoped to see again this side of eternity.

"Val!" Boy Justice shouted in ecstasy. "You're alive!"

"I do wish you wouldn't use that diminutive of my name, young fellow," said the Blue Valentine. "Rather tends to undercut my dignity."

The Valentine put the match to one of the torches and then, flipping open his sterling silver cigarette case with an elegant gesture, he withdrew one of the black Russian cigarettes he favoured and lit it from the flame of the torch.

"But how…?" Boy Justice uttered in confusion. "You were…"

The Valentine smiled, and held out the now-closed cigarette case in order to let Boy Justice see the flattened bullet embedded in the centre of its filigree design.

"Lined with adamantium," he said. "And always worn over my heart."

In the same movement that replaced the case in his inside pocket, the Valentine produced another blue domino mask and affixed it to his face. "I don't suppose you happened to notice my topper anywhere before that rather melodramatic dousing of the lights?" he said.

Boy Justice, still reeling from the shock of his mentor's rebirth, pointed to where the blue silk opera hat lay on the stone floor.

"Well spotted, sir," said the Valentine and, retrieving the hat, placed it atop his head at the slightly rakish angle he preferred.

"Better?" he said.

"Better," the lad replied.

The Valentine put out his hand, and Boy Justice, returning the gesture, gripped it fervently.

"The Oath?" he asked.

"The Oath," said the Valentine, and, together, they repeated the words that had come to be feared by wrongdoers everywhere:

Where Evil lurks, it shall not live;

The Valentine does not forgive.

The Valentine nodded, smiled, and removed the flaming torch from its wall-holder. "The work awaits," he said. "Let us explore the labyrinth. We have criminals to kill, and innocents to rescue." With no further ado, the Blue Valentine set out beneath one of the vaulted arches to whatever mysteries lay beyond.

Boy Justice stared after him, watching until the midnight blue of the Valentine's costume could no longer be distinguished from the shadows surrounding it. Any moment now, the lad thought. Any moment now, I'll start after him. Yes. Any moment now. But why weren't his legs moving? Why did he suddenly feel so tired, so weak, so old? Why couldn't he open his mouth to call after his friend?

Without understanding why, he felt his thumb rubbing against the first two fingers of his hand. The fingers that had worked the padlock – the padlock that had been coated with a mysterious oily substance...

Poison!

Boy Justice tried to shout, tried to move, but it was too late. He was powerless against the sudden wave of dizzying unconsciousness that raced through his body, slamming into him like a tight little fist that drove him to the floor and dropped him into blackness.

~~~

Alderton blinked his eyes open.

A grinning face was looking down at him.

"How'd *that* feel, Pops?" Irish said.

Alderton, still on his back on the floor, opened his mouth to answer but started spluttering on the blood that flowed in from his shattered nose. He felt like he was going to choke, felt the accompanying panic rise, and forced himself to take slow shallow breaths until his body decided it wasn't going to die right that minute. He twisted his head on the floor to look around.

He couldn't have been out long because nothing else seemed to have happened. The kid was still huddled, petrified, on the chair, and KGB was still standing a few feet behind Irish, passing the time by doing a little browsing of Alderton's poorly stocked bookshelf. He ran a finger along the spines of the thrift-store paperbacks as he turned to look down at Alderton.

"You read all these?" he asked.

All these? Christ almighty, there were probably twenty-five books in total. "No," Alderton said. "I just keep them there to impress my dates." He finally managed to get himself up onto one elbow. "Little help here?" he said to Irish, extending his other hand for a lift.

"Fuckoff," Irish said.

Nice. Alderton grabbed at his stick, lying beside him, to help himself up but Irish snatched it away from him. "Don't want you getting ambitious," he said, and broke the stick in two over his knee, letting the broken halves fall back to the floor.

"Huh?" Alderton said, then got it. "Oh, right," he said, picking up the longer half of the broken stick, and levering himself awkwardly up on to one knee. "Your chosen profession has taught you to exercise caution, even in the least likely of situations."

Irish curled his lip. "Speak fucking English," he said.

"You're being careful," Alderton said. "Perfectly understandable. You're fearful, lest an old cripple give you a nasty tap with a thin piece of wood."

KGB laughed, with what sounded like actual pleasure. "*Lest,*" he said, voice cracking on the word with amused delight. Alderton had always enjoyed an appreciative audience, but he wished KGB had kept his admiration to himself. Because Irish plainly felt slighted by his partner's laughter, felt a tiny slip in his command of the room, and was going to have to do something about that.

He glared at Alderton. "You think you're better

than me?" he said.

Alderton – still on one knee, his arm trembling as it tried to lift his miserable old body, the shattered end of the broken walking stick all but buckling on the floor – stared up at him, at the rage in his dark little eyes, and saw the future. Saw the absence of reason, the absence of mercy, saw himself and the kid dead at the hands of this stupid thug, and thought fuck it.

"Better than you?" he said. "I've passed *turds* that are better than you, you rancid little motherfucker."

Irish's face creased in primal fury and he flung himself down toward Alderton.

Moron, Alderton thought, and wished he had time to say it.

But he didn't. What he had time to do was raise the stick and keep it as stiff as his atrophied muscles allowed.

The idiot's momentum did the rest. The sharp end of the shattered walking stick slid easily through his left eye and plunged deep inside his skull. Alderton gave a further twisting thrust until he knew he'd skewered the fucker's brain and then flipped the body aside.

"Jesus Christ!" KGB shouted, shock freezing him in place. "Alan!"

Alan? The fuck kind of gangster name was that? Alderton watched KGB finally raise his hands into fists like he was going to do something. But KGB wasn't going to do shit. Alderton was. He reached over Alan's twitching body and yanked the gun out of his waistband.

KGB was running at him now, but Alderton felt like he had all the time in the world. Too young for Korea, too old for Vietnam, but two years in the service and plenty of target practice. He cocked the gun, held his breath, and fired.

Like riding a fucking bike. The bullet went exactly where Alderton wanted. KGB's kneecap exploded in a shower of blood and bone and Alderton watched him hit the floor screaming.

Behind him, he heard the kid exhale loudly, part gasp, part sigh of relief, and Alderton forced himself upright with the other half of his stick. He limped a step or two toward KGB. Fuck the limp. Fuck Time's fleet-foot run to the grave. Fuck everything, especially this whimpering bully and his dead or dying asshole friend. Alderton's blood was up and something resembling the memory of an erection was stirring in his pants. He levelled the gun in the direction of KGB's face and watched him splutter and sob.

"Georgie Balloons," Alderton said. "Joey Rats. Those are fucking gangster names, you pissant little bitch."

His finger tightened on the trigger.

KGB closed his eyes in terror.

The Valentine does not forgive, said a voice in Alderton's head. The kid's voice. Brooks Barrett's voice. The voice of Alderton's rage at all that had been lost. The voice of the dark. The voice of the Valentine himself, primal and merciless.

But the Valentine wasn't here. It wasn't his call anymore.

Alderton waited a moment. Took a breath. Let the adrenaline rush recede.

KGB opened his eyes, squinting, unsure, afraid to hope.

Alderton lowered the gun. Slightly. "One word," he said. "One wrong move."

KGB nodded, carefully.

"Call the cops, kid," Alderton said. "Use that fancy phone of yours. Use a fucking app, if you like. Knock yourself out."

But the kid wasn't listening. *"Boy Justice,"* he was whispering. *"Boy Justice."* Like a mantra. Like a prayer. Like everything he'd needed to be true in the world suddenly was.

~~~

Later, after the cops had come and gone and a woman from Social Services was on her way to take the kid home, the kid asked Alderton what happened now.

"You go home to your mother," Alderton said.

"She's not my mother."

"Does she feed you?"

"Yeah."

"Wash your clothes? Get you to school on time?"

A shrug, a reluctant nod.

"She ever smack you around?"

"No."

"Then she's meeting minimum requirements," Alderton said. "The rest of it you're going to have to find for yourself. It's there if you look. Be good to your friends. If they're not good to you, find better friends."

"Most of my friends are idiots," the kid said.

"That's life in the big city."

The kid cocked his head, looked at Alderton appraisingly. "You're quoting *Robocop*," he said.

"Oh," Alderton said. "Check out the big brain on Brad."

"*Pulp Fiction*," the kid said.

"See?" said Alderton. "Not *all* your friends are idiots."

The kid just looked at him. Life had already taught the poor little bastard not to ask.

"Saturday afternoons," Alderton said. "Provided it's alright with your mother. We'll watch movies, get drunk, and smoke cigarettes."

The kid's mouth fell open.

"Jesus," Alderton said. "What are you, retarded? No booze, no cigarettes. Learn to recognise a joke, for Christ's sake."

The kid smiled at him.

Alderton felt his heart jump in his chest. Not the arrhythmia for once, thank Christ, but something older, something waking from a long sleep.

He hoped that somewhere, in whatever unlikely area of heaven God reserved for people born not of flesh and blood but of imagination and desire, the Blue Valentine was proud of him. *The work awaits,* he'd said in Alderton's dream. *We have criminals to kill, and innocents to rescue.*

Well, it was going to be slow, and it was unlikely to be spectacular, but a rescue was nevertheless underway.

As he felt his own mouth return the kid's smile, though, Alderton found himself wondering just for a moment which of them it was who was being rescued.

OF SHADOWS, OF LIGHT AND DARK

Jo Fletcher

Life is a dream,
A nightmare,
A *mélange*
Of shadows, of light and dark.

A series of passions
And tears
And promises:
Shadows, both light and dark.

Leaps of elation,
Then sloughs
Of despond
Cast shadows of light and dark.

Glorious triumphs,
Defeats
And disasters,
All shadows, all light and dark.

Life is a mystery,
Misery,
Mazery,
Shadows of light and dark.

ALCHEMY PRESS PUBLICATIONS

We'll Always Have Alchemy ed Peter Coleborn (2024)

Of Sands and Tides by Jan Edwards (2024)

The Alchemy Press Book of the Dead 2023 by Stephen Jones (2024, co-published with Phantasmagoria Publications)

Tournament of Shadows by Pauline E Dungate (2023)

The Gogamagog Circus by Garry Kilworth (2023)

The Alchemy Press Book of the Dead 2022 by Stephen Jones (2023)

Let Your Hinged Jaw Do the Talking by Tom Johnstone (2022

The Alchemy Press Book of the Dead 2021 by Stephen Jones (2022)

The Alchemy Press Book of Horrors 3 ed Peter Coleborn & Jan Edwards (2021)

The Alchemy Press Book of the Dead 2020 by Stephen Jones (2021)

A Small Thing for Yolanda by Jan Edwards (2020)

Les Vacances by Phil Sloman (2020)

Talking to Strangers and Other Warnings by Tina Rath (2020)

The Alchemy Press Book of Horrors 2 ed Peter Coleborn & Jan Edwards (2020)

Compromising the Truth by Bryn Fortey (2018)

The Alchemy Press Book of Horrors ed Peter Coleborn & Jan Edwards (2018)

The Complete Weird Epistles of Penelope Pettiweather by Jessica Amanda Salmonson (2016)

The Private Life of Elder Things by Adrian Tchaikovsky, Adam Gauntlett & Keris McDonald (2016)

Something Remains ed Peter Coleborn & Pauline E Dungate (2016)

Dead Water and Other Weird Tales by David A Sutton (2015)

Give Me These Moments Back by Mike Chinn (2015)

Leinster Gardens and Other Subtleties by Jan Edwards (2015)

Monsters by Paul Kane (2015)

Evocations by James Brogden (2015)

Music in the Bone by Marion Pitman (2015)

Music From the Fifth Planet by Anne Nicholls (2015)

Kneeling in the Silver Light ed by Dean M Drinkel (2014)

Nick Nightmare Investigates by Adrian Cole (2014 co-published with Airgedlāmh Publications)

The Alchemy Press Book of Pulp Heroes 3 ed Mike Chinn (2014)

The Alchemy Press Book of Urban Mythic 2 ed Jan Edwards & Jenny Barber (2014)

Tell No Lies by John Grant (2014)

Merry-Go-Round and Other Words by Bryn Fortey (2014)

Touchstones: Essays on the Fantastic by John Howard (2014)

Astrologica: Stories of the Zodiac ed Allen Ashley (2013)

The Alchemy Press Book of Pulp Heroes 2 ed Mike Chinn (2013)

The Alchemy Press Book of Urban Mythic ed Jan Edwards & Jenny Barber (2013)

Invent-10n by Rod Rees (2013)

In the Broken Birdcage of Kathleen Fair by Cate Gardner (2013 online)

The Komarovs by Chico Kidd (2013 online)

Doors to Elsewhere by Mike Barrett (2013)

Sex, Lies and Family Ties by Sarah J Graham (2012)

The Alchemy Press Book of Ancient Wonders ed Jan Edwards and Jenny Barber (2012)

The Alchemy Press Book of Pulp Heroes ed Mike Chinn (2012)

Sailor of the Skies by Mike Chinn (2011 online)

Rumours of the Marvellous by Peter Atkins (2011 co-published with Airgedlámh Publications)

Beneath the Ground ed Joel Lane (2003)

Swords Against the Millennium ed Mike Chinn (2000 co-published with Saladoth Productions)

Where the Bodies are Buried by Kim Newman (2000 co-published with Airgedlámh Publications)

Shadows of Light and Dark by Jo Fletcher (1998 co-published with Airgedlámh Publications)

The Paladin Mandates by Mike Chinn (1998)

Cover art by (clockwise
from top left): Bob
Covington, Stephen
Cooney, Clive Barker
and David A Hardy

AUTHORS AND ARTISTS

A massive Thank You to all the artists and writers and editors who have worked with us to produce over 25 years of amazing books. Hats off to:

Colleen Anderson, Gail-Nina Anderson, Sarah Ash,
Allen Ashley, Peter Atkins, Simon Avery,
Stephen Bacon, Ben Baldwin, Jenny Barber,
Suzanne Barbieri, Carl Barker, Clive Barker,
Mike Barrett, Debbie Bennett, Simon Bestwick,
Doug Blakeslee, Randy Broecker, James Brogden,
Rupert Brooke, Gary Budgen, Mark David Campbell,
Ramsey Campbell, Dave Carson, Mike Chinn,
Joyce Chng, Zen Cho, Ray Cluley, Lynn M Cochrane,
Adrian Cole, Storm Constantine, Stephen Cooney,
Andrew Coulthard, Gary Couzens, Bob Covington,
Adam Craig, Peter Crowther, K T Davies,
Aliette de Bodard, Rima Devereaux, Evan Dicken,
Sarah Doyle, Dean M Drinkel, Pauline E Dungate,
Graham Edwards, Jan Edwards, Les Edwards,
Paul Edwards, Bob Eggleton, Stephanie Ellis,
Jaine Fenn, Paul Finch, Jo Fletcher, Bryn Fortey,
Christopher Fowler, Milo James Fowler, Derek Fox,
David Jón Fuller, Neil Gaiman, Cate Gardner,
Liam Garriock, Martin Gateley, Adam Gauntlett,
Christopher Golden, Sharon Gosling, Jason Gould,

John Grant, James Gregory, Kate Griffin,
Terry Grimwood, Shaun A J Hamilton,
Anthony Hanks, David A Hardy, Dominic Harman,
Nancy Hayden, James Hartley, Michael Haynes,
Misha Herwin, Andrew Hook, Amber L Husbands,
Glen Hirshberg, John Howard, Ian Hunter,
Chris Iovenko, Robert William Iveniuk, Tim Jeffreys,
Tom Johnstone, Matt Joiner, Stephen Jones,
Emile-Louis Tomas Jouvet, Paul Kane,
Eyglo Karlsdottir, Megan Kerr, Chico Kidd,
Nancy Kilpatrick, Garry Kilworth, Joel Lane,
Stephen Laws, Tim Lebbon, Samantha Lee, Tanith Lee,
D F Lewis, Alison Littlewood, Bob Lock, Selina Lock,
Simon Macculloch, Bracken MacLeod, Johnny Mains,
David Mathew, Peter Mark May, Jet McDonald,
Keris McDonald, David McGoarty, Mike McKeown,
Gary McMahon, William Meikle, Adam Millard,
Edward Miller, Ralph Robert Moore, Chris Morgan,
Christine Morgan, Lou Morgan, Pauline Morgan,
Kim Newman, Anne Nicholls, Stan Nicholls,
Thana Niveau, Jonathan Oliver, Marie O'Regan,
Marion Pitman, Jim Pitts, John Llewellyn Probert,
Rosanne Rabinowitz, Madhvi Ramani, Tina Rath,
Chris Rawlins, Rod Rees, Mike Resnick, Tony Richards,
David A Riley, Justina Robson, Nicholas Royle,
Lynda E Rucker, Daniel I Russell, Seamus A Ryan,
Jessica Amanda Salmonson, Steven Savile,
Gaie Sebold, Daniele Serra, Ralph Sevush,
Christopher Shy, Phil Sloman, Michael Marshall Smith,

Karri Sperring, Paul Starkey, Sylvia Starshine,
Thomas Strømsholt, David A Sutton, Peter Sutton,
Adrian Tchaikovsky, Steve Rasnic Tem,
David Thomas, David Turnbull, Steve Upham,
Mark Valentine, Nicholas Vince, K T Wagner,
Ian Whates, Arch Whitehouse, Neil Williamson,
Shannon Connor Winward, Joshua Wolf,
Ashe Woodward, Paul Woodward, Joe X Young,
Stuart Young.

If I have missed anyone, I sincerely apologise.

Printed in Great Britain
by Amazon